A TWIST IN TIME

Cosy Walker is having a difficult time. Her mum has gone into hospital and Cosy has been sent to stay with foster parents. The other girls being fostered, Jade and Jemma, think she's a snob because she's won a scholarship to the high school. Cosy's got problems there as well. She's finding it hard to settle and to cope with the homework—maths especially. Then she makes a startling discovery: her room is haunted! Strangely, Cosy isn't frightened –she finds the ghost girl rather comforting. She is like a friend, a kindred spirit, sitting at her desk, writing in her diary of a ghost girl that she has seen—a ghost girl who bears a strong resemblance to Cosy. Somehow, a twist in time has allowed the girls to see into each other's lives . . .

A TWIST
IN TIME

Jean Ure

First published in 2000 by
Walker Books Ltd
This Large Print edition published by
BBC Audiobooks by arrangement with
Walker Books Ltd 2006

ISBN 10: 1 4056 6073 2
ISBN 13: 978 1 4056 6073 0

British Library Cataloguing in Publication Data available

20033689

Printed and bound in Great Britain by
Antony Rowe Ltd., Chippenham, Wiltshire

*In fondest memory
of Wendy*

CHAPTER ONE

When Cosy Walker's mum went into hospital, Cosy had nowhere to go. She hadn't any family. No grandparents, no aunties or uncles. Not even a dad. Cosy's dad had died when she was eight years old. Now she was eleven. Well, eleven and almost a half. But even eleven and a half was too young to be on her own. The lady at the Town Hall, Miss Marriott, said she would have to be fostered.

'We've found a family for you to live with. Just until your mum comes back.'

She didn't say when that was likely to be, and Cosy was too scared to ask. Weeks? Months? *Years?*

Maybe never.

Never was too frightening! Cosy couldn't bring herself to think of never.

'Couldn't I stay with Mrs Pink?' she said. Mrs Pink was the lady who owned the house where Cosy and her mum had a flat. Mrs Pink lived downstairs and Cosy and her mum lived upstairs.

'Mrs Pink would have me!' said Cosy.

But Miss Marriott said that Mrs Pink was too old.

'I stayed with her before,' said Cosy, 'when Mum had to go into hospital.'

'Yes, Cosy, I know you did, but . . . that was a bit different.'

'How was it different?'

'Well, for one thing, Mrs Pink was younger. And for another—' Miss Marriott paused.

'What?' said Cosy.

'For another,' said Miss Marriott, putting her arm round Cosy's shoulders, 'that was only for a couple of weeks.'

So then Cosy knew that she had been right not to ask Miss Marriott how long. If it was going to be longer than last time, then she definitely didn't want to know.

Miss Marriott had come to Grange Park to collect Cosy and take her to the new family. Grange Park was where Mrs Pink had her house. The new family lived in Dornton Heath. That was miles away! Right over on the

2

other side of town. A whole different world. Cosy had heard bad things about Dornton Heath. It was where rough people lived, and gangs of youths. She didn't want to go there!

Mrs Pink didn't want her to go there, either. She cried as Cosy and Miss Marriott came downstairs carrying Cosy's bags.

'I'm going to miss you,' she said.

'I'm going to miss you!' cried Cosy.

She always thought of Mrs Pink as a kind of gran.

'The house is going to seem so empty . . . I shan't know what to do with myself!'

'At least you'll still have Jonathan,' said Cosy.

Jonathan was Mrs Pink's cat. A big ginger fluffball. He came and rubbed against Cosy, purring his farewells. Cosy blinked back tears. Mrs Pink would have Jonathan. Cosy wouldn't have anyone! She was being sent to live with strangers.

'The Ridleys are lovely people,' said Miss Marriott as she bundled Cosy's bags into the back of the car. 'You'll like it with them.'

Cosy scrubbed at her eyes. She wouldn't like it! She would hate it! She didn't want to go! And what kind of a name was *Wriggly*? Ugh! They sounded like a family of worms.

'There are two other girls being fostered with them,' said Miss Marriott. 'Jade and Jemma. About the same age as you. They're a lively pair!'

The news sunk Cosy into further gloom. She hadn't realized there would be other girls. She wasn't used to having to mix. She was used to being an only child! She enjoyed being on her own.

'Do they go to my school?'

'No, they go to Hall Cross. I'm sorry, Cosy, it's going to be rather a long journey for you, across town. But it's only one bus, so you should be able to cope.'

From Grange Park, Cosy had been able to walk to school. Lots of the girls lived in Grange Park. She bet none of them lived in Dornton Heath!

'How are you getting on there, anyway?' said Miss Marriott.

'All right, thank you.' Cosy said it politely.

'Do you think you're going to like it?'

She *had* thought she was going to like it. Earlier in the year, when she'd heard she'd won the scholarship. Mum had been so excited!

'Oh, Cosy! Isn't it wonderful? All our hard work has paid off!'

Mum had helped Cosy. They had studied together. Cosy couldn't have done it without Mum. She remembered the day she'd gone into town with Mrs Pink, to Maplin's, the big department store, to buy her uniform. Blue pleated skirt, cream blouse, navy sweater . . . how she had peacocked when she got back home! Parading round the sitting-room, showing off to Mum.

Mum had been so proud of her! She'd been so looking forward to Cosy's first day. Cosy had been looking forward to coming home and telling Mum all about it. Mum always loved to hear what was happening in the outside world—the world she could never go into. Cosy wasn't quite sure *why* her mum couldn't go into it; just that she couldn't. It scared her, it upset her. So Mum stayed indoors and waited for Cosy to tell her all the things that were going on.

But she'd never heard about Cosy's first day. Cosy had got home to find that her mum had been rushed into hospital.

'Poor soul! Poor soul!' said Mrs Pink, who had gone with her in the ambulance. 'She never meant to do it!'

Cosy's mum had taken too many of her tablets. And now she had to stay in hospital in case she did it again.

But she wouldn't, thought Cosy, *if only I could be with her all the time!* But Cosy had to go to school. If Mum thought Cosy was missing out on school it would make her unhappy.

'It's such a shame,' said Miss Marriott. 'Your very first week! It's been a really disturbed start for you, hasn't it?'

'It's not Mum's fault,' said Cosy. 'She couldn't help it.'

Cosy was fiercely protective of her

mum. She knew people thought she was weird, never leaving the house, but she and Cosy managed to have fun. They did lots of reading together and played lots of games and watched their favourite videos. When Mum wasn't depressed she and Cosy really enjoyed themselves.

'Here we are,' said Miss Marriott. 'Alma Road.'

To Cosy's surprise, Alma Road had trees in it. She hadn't thought there would be any trees in Dornton Heath. She hadn't thought it was that sort of place. She studied the houses as they drove past. Most of them seemed to be old, and some of them were quite large—well, large compared to Mrs Pink's, which was ordinary and modern and the same as all its neighbours.

Number 44 was one of the quite large ones. It looked a bit dark and spooky to Cosy. It had a yew tree in the front garden and stained glass panels in the front door. And chimney pots! Sticking up like fingers out of the roof. Cosy had never lived in a house with chimney pots. Chimney pots were *really*

7

old.

Miss Marriott led the way up the path, which was made of bricks and was all overgrown with green weedy things pushing through the cracks. *Run down*, thought Cosy. She was determined not to like this horrible place, even if it did have chimney pots.

A big fat woman with arms the size of Cosy didn't know what, arms like blown-up *sausages*, was standing beaming at the front door. She might have looked warm and cushiony and welcoming if Cosy hadn't made up her mind to hate everything.

'Hello! Is this Cosy?' she said.

'This is Cosy,' agreed Miss Marriott. 'Cosy, this is Mrs Ridley.'

'Call me Auntie,' said Mrs Wriggly. 'They all do! Come on in, Cosy, and meet the gang.'

The gang were the two girls, Jemma and Jade, and Mrs Wriggly's husband, Mr Wriggly. Mr Wriggly was tall and thin with a face that looked as if it had spent its life being walked into brick walls. All craggy and cracked and lined.

'He's the guv'nor,' said Mrs Wriggly.

8

'You can call him Guv . . . Isn't that right, girls?'

Jade and Jemma giggled, as if at some private joke.

'He's the Guv,' they agreed.

'So-called,' said Mr Wriggly. 'You'll find, Cosy, that I have very little say what goes on in this place.' He winked at Jade and Jemma. 'That's about the size of it, wouldn't you say?'

At this the girls giggled again and Mrs Wriggly said, 'Oh, get away with you!' and flapped at Mr Wriggly with a tea towel. 'Come upstairs, Cosy, love, and we'll show you where you're going to be. Are you coming with us, you two?'

Everyone except Mr Wriggly trooped up the stairs. Cosy could feel the girls eyeing her. She was eyeing them, as well. Jade—she thought it was Jade—had green eyes like a cat's and long red hair. Jemma had freckles and a turned-up nose. Jade looked rather fierce: Jemma looked impish. They were both bigger and stronger than Cosy, who was small for her age and rather pale, with hair that couldn't make up its mind whether to be brown or mouse but which in any case was wispy. Jade's hair was thick and heavy and Jemma's hair had a bounce, but Cosy's hung dismally straight and made her face, she thought, look like a pudding.

You couldn't have much confidence when you looked like a pudding. Not even if you had been clever enough to win a scholarship to the high school.

'Well!' said Miss Marriott. 'What do you think of your bedroom, Cosy?'

Cosy looked round, shyly. 'It's nice.'

It *was* nice. Even a person who had made up her mind to hate everything couldn't deny that it was nice. It had a real old-fashioned fireplace with pretty pink-gold paper on the walls and crimson curtains at the window. Cosy, thought Cosy, and immediately wished that she hadn't.

'Cosy likes to be cosy!' That had been one of her mum's jokes.

'We've given you a table, look!' said Mrs Wriggly. 'We thought you'd like somewhere quiet, for your homework.'

Cosy nodded, gratefully. They had a *lot* of homework, at the high school.

She had only been there a week, but she had already discovered that. And Mum not there to help her!

'Well, now, you've got the weekend to get settled,' said Miss Marriott as she prepared to leave. 'I'll call by next Friday and see how you're getting on. Any problems, just tell Mrs Ridley. All right?'

'Yes.' It wasn't all right, it was horrible. Being left with strangers! But there didn't seem much point in saying so. They weren't going to let her go home.

'So, now! What would you like to do?' said Mrs Wriggly when the front door had closed behind Miss Marriott, leaving Cosy a prisoner. 'Stay down here and get to know the others, or do a bit of unpacking before supper?'

'Do a bit of unpacking,' mumbled Cosy.

'Righty-oh, then! You go up and get all your things put away, and I'll give you a yell when supper's ready, or you just come down when you've finished. Whichever.'

Cosy didn't have very much in the

11

way of unpacking. Just two small suitcases full of clothes, and a holdall with some of the things she couldn't bear to be parted from. Her favourite books and pictures, her china ornaments, a carved wooden box containing what Mum called her 'trinkets', a Spanish doll that her dad had brought back with him from a business trip. And, of course, a photograph of Mum. Not that she could ever forget what Mum looked like! But she wanted her to be there, by the side of the bed, so that she could kiss her good night every evening before going to sleep and again every morning when she woke up.

She had just about finished arranging her ornaments on the mantelshelf when there was a knock at the door and Jade and Jemma came bounding in.

'Hi,' said Jemma.

'Hi,' said Jade.

'Is it OK if we come in?'

They already were in.

'We've come to tell you about us.'

'We're cousins, see?'

Jade plonked herself down on Cosy's bed. Jemma perched on the edge of the table. Cosy stood by the fireplace, clasping a china pig.

'We thought you ought to know, if you're going to live with us.' It was Jade who took up the story. 'See, Jem used to live with her mum and dad. Right? But then her mum ran away and left her, and her dad went and shacked up with this other woman and Jem didn't get on with her, did you?'

'Didn't get on with her,' agreed Jemma, swinging her legs.

'Horrible cow, she was. No one could stand her. So Jem come to live with us. Me and my mum. Which was all right.'

'Yeah, it was! It was all right.'

'Till *my* mum got this other bloke and he was, like, pushing us about all the time. Know what I mean?'

Cosy didn't. She said, 'Um—'

'Coming on really heavy, you know?'

'We got so's we couldn't stand it.'

'Couldn't stand it,' said Jemma.

'So know what we done? Tell her what we done!'

13

'We run away,' said Jemma.

'Went down London. Took 'em three weeks to suss us out.'

'Three weeks,' said Jemma.

Cosy listened in growing wonderment.

'Had the cops after us an' all. An' when they got us, we swore we wasn't never going back.'

'Never,' said Jemma.

'Not so long as her bloke's there. We told 'em, we'd just run off again. So that's when they put us with Auntie and Guv.'

'They're ace,' said Jemma.

'They are. They're ace. We bin with 'em—how long we bin with 'em?'

'Six months, near enough.'

'Six months.'

Jade looked at Cosy, as if expecting some sort of comment.

'Gosh,' said Cosy.

'Gosh.' Jemma gave a loud shriek of laughter.

'What about you?' said Jade. 'What you doing here?'

Cosy took a breath. She pushed a wisp of hair behind her ear.

'My mum's in hospital and there's nowhere else I can go.'

'Why? Where's your dad? Did he run off, like Jemma's mum?'

'No. He died.'

'Tough,' said Jade.

'Not as tough as if he'd run off,' said Jemma. 'Not like he just abandoned her.'

Jade said, 'Shut up! She don't need that.'

'Neither did I,' said Jemma.

'Look, just shut *up*, will ya? We done our bit. It's her turn, now.' Jade slewed round to face Cosy. 'So what's the matter with your mum? She got cancer or something?'

'No!' Cosy was horrified. What a thing to say!

'So what's wrong with her?'

'She's just . . . not very well.'

'Why? Is she a PA?'

Cosy put a finger to her mouth and tore at a piece of skin. Jemma gave another of her loud cackles.

'She don't know what a PA is!'

Jade kindly explained. 'It means someone who drinks too much.'

'My mum never drinks anything!' said Cosy. Only a glass of sherry at Christmas, with Mrs Pink. Surely that didn't make her a PA?

'So what's her problem? I s'ppose she's a junkie.'

Cosy's face grew a bit pink. She knew what a junkie was. At least, she thought she did.

'Drug addict,' said Jemma, just in case she didn't.

'You don't have to get all red,' said Jade. 'Not your fault.'

'But she isn't a junkie!' said Cosy. 'She's just not very strong. Life gets too much for her.' That's what Mrs Pink had said. There were times when life got too much and Cosy's mum couldn't cope. Then she had to go into hospital for a bit until she felt better. 'She gets all right again. For a little while.'

'Way out!' said Jemma.

'It's not her fault! She can't help it.'

'Well, never mind about that,' said Jade. 'What's all this with the table?'

She waved her hand towards it.

'It's for my homework,' said Cosy.

'What do you want a table for your

homework for? We ain't got no table for homework.'

'We don't do no homework.' Jemma giggled. 'Not if we can help it!'

'I have to.' Cosy explained it, earnestly. 'You get into trouble if you don't.'

'Why?' Jade regarded her, suspiciously. 'Where'd you go to school?'

'I just started. At the high school.'

'Oh! The snob school.'

'It's not snobby,' said Cosy. 'It's just that you have to work really hard.'

'Snobby swot school!'

'Where'd your mum get the money to send you there?' Jemma had stopped swinging her legs. She suddenly sounded quite aggressive. 'She come into a fortune, or something?'

'I won a scholarship.' Cosy said it apologetically, as if winning a scholarship was something to be ashamed of. But she didn't want them getting the wrong idea and thinking she was rich and privileged. She had a feeling they wouldn't like her if they

17

thought that.

They weren't going to like her anyway.

'What I said.' Jade tapped her forehead. 'Snobby swot.'

'Well, with a name like Co-zee . . . What kind of a name's that s'pposed to be?'

'It's Italian,' said Cosy. 'It's short for Cosima.'

'You ain't Italian!'

'No, but my gran was.' Granny Cosy; Mum's mum. Granny Teacosy, Mum had called her. If Granny Teacosy had been alive, Cosy could have gone and stayed with her instead of being left in this dark spooky old house with these angry shouting girls who plainly thought she was a complete nerd. *And* a snobby swot.

Auntie's voice came bawling up the stairs. She had a big voice, to match her big body.

'Girls! Supper's on the table!'

'That's it,' said Jade, springing off the bed. 'Nosh time!'

Jade and Jemma disappeared. Cosy heard their footsteps thudding down

18

the stairs. The reason they thudded was that the stairs didn't have proper stair carpet, just some tatty sort of lino stuff.

At Mrs Pink's there had been real stair carpet.

Cosy felt her eyes begin to prick. She went over to the bed and picked up her photograph of Mum. Darling Mum! So little and sweet and fragile. She pressed the photograph to her lips.

'Please, Mum,' whispered Cosy, 'get better *soon*!'

CHAPTER TWO

Saturday morning, a week later. Cosy had lived with the Wrigglys for seven whole days. (She had discovered that their name was Ridley, but she still thought of them as the Wrigglys.) Jade and Jemma were jostling for position in the bathroom.

'Get out the way! I was here first!'

'You get out the way! And stop shoving at me, you fat cow! That was my eye you just stuck your elbow in!'

'Well, move over, then! Or I'll gob toothpaste at you!'

Cosy, who had been in the bathroom before either of them, hastily ducked as a glob of toothpaste came flying towards her.

'Filthy pig!' screeched Jade. She snatched at a toothbrush and swooshed it in the hand basin. 'Take that!'

'Yeeeurgh!'

Jemma shrieked as a tidal wave of water came washing over her. Cosy grabbed a towel. Jade was always so *vigorous*. Whatever she did, she did it ten times louder and more energetically than anyone else. In some ways, Cosy envied her.

'Whose brush is this, anyway?'

'Actually,' said Cosy, 'it's mine.'

'ECKtewlly,' said Jemma, 'it's *mane*.'

Cosy felt her cheeks grow pink. She hated it when they imitated her.

'You don't half talk prissy,' said Jemma.

'I can't help it.'

'Ay cahn't help it!'

Cosy hung the towel back on its rail

and hurried from the bathroom. She was going to start crying. It was awful! She *kept* crying. The least little thing set her off. But it was horrid of them to mock her! It wasn't her fault she talked the way she did. Mum had always insisted that she speak nicely. They'd read poems together. *The Pied Piper of Hamelin, The Highwayman, Jabberwocky.*

'I want you to have every opportunity, sweetheart! I don't want to mess up your life the way I've messed up mine.'

Cosy blotted at her eyes. Jade and Jemma already thought she was a complete nerd. She didn't want them to know she'd been crying.

They had abandoned their battle for the bathroom and were already downstairs, clattering about the kitchen while Auntie cooked breakfast.

'Look!' Jemma had picked up a copy of the local free paper. 'Look at this!'

'What?' Jade craned over her shoulder.

'Darren Walsh!'

'Where?'

'Here!'

'Where?'

Jemma stabbed a finger on to the page. 'See?'

'What's he doing?'

'Says he's going to open the Chocolate Shop.'

'What Chocolate Shop?'

Jemma peered closer at the page. 'The Arcades. Waddington. Says he's going to be there at eleven o'clock. *Auntie!*' Jemma spun round. 'Can we go?'

'I expect you might be able to. You'll have to ask the guv'nor.'

Auntie always said they would have to ask the guv'nor. But everyone knew that it was Auntie's word that counted. If she said something was all right, then it was all right.

'Darren *Walsh!*' Jade and Jemma threw up their hands and screamed.

'Who is he, anyway?' said Auntie.

They stared at her in disbelief. 'He's Wacko!'

'And who's Wacko when he's at home?'

'Wacko in *The B Team!*'

How could anyone not know that? Even Cosy knew it!

'Here's the guv'nor,' said Auntie. 'See if he'll let you go.'

'Guv!' Jade and Jemma went howling across the kitchen. 'Is it all right if we go into Waddington to see Darren Walsh?'

Of course Guv said it was. There weren't many things that were banned in the Wriggly household. Staying out late was one. Going somewhere without saying where was another. Swearing was another. These were about the only rules that Cosy had been able to make out. And even then Jade and Jemma didn't take much notice of rule number three. They were always using words that would have made Miss Addison, Cosy's form mistress at the high school, turn purple in the face. They were very strict about language at the high school.

Auntie would just say mildly, 'No swearing, please, girls.' It wasn't any wonder, thought Cosy, that Jade and Jemma didn't take any notice of her. If anyone swore in Miss Addison's hearing there would be *real* trouble.

'How about if I drive you in?' said Guv. 'Only you'll have to make your own way back. That sound OK?'

'Brilliant!' Jade jumped up and punched the air.

'We might even get his autograph,' breathed Jemma.

'How about Cosy?' Guv ruffled her wispy hair. 'Does she want to go and get his autograph?'

Cosy opened her mouth to say yes— and then stopped. At the mention of her name, Jade and Jemma exchanged glances. Jemma had pulled a face. Jade had turned down the corners of her mouth. They couldn't have made it more obvious that they didn't want her. On the other hand . . . Darren Walsh! Imagine seeing him as he really was! She and Mum had always watched the soaps together. *The B Team* was one of their favourites; and Darren Walsh was everyone's dream! Well, not Auntie's perhaps, but Auntie was old. Heaps older than Mum. Mum was still quite young and pretty. Cosy would love to be able to tell her that she had actually seen Darren Walsh!

'Is Cosy a fan, as well?' said Guv.

Jade's lip curled. 'She probably don't even know who he is!'

'I do!' said Cosy. She couldn't let that pass. Darren Walsh was one of her claims to fame. Her *only* claim to fame. 'His brother used to go to my school.'

'Oh, yeah?' They didn't believe her. How could a nerd like Cosy Walker have gone to the same school as Darren Walsh's brother?

'What school was that, then? Saint Posho's?'

'Belvedere Juniors.'

'Oh! *Belvedeah!*' They were at it again. Mocking her.

'It was just an ordinary school,' protested Cosy.

'So what was Darren Walsh's brother doing there?'

'It's where Darren Walsh used to go.'

They looked at her, eyes narrowed.

'What's his name?' Jade challenged her. 'Tell us his name!'

'Michael Bone.'

'Michael *Bone*? How come he's Michael Bone?'

' 'Cos that's Darren Walsh's real name . . . Darren Walsh is his *stage* name.'

'So there!' said Auntie. 'Now you know.'

They couldn't very well not take her with them after that.

Guv drove them in and left them at the entrance to the Arcades.

'Be back in time for lunch,' he said.

'Yeah. Right. Hey! There's Dee and Kristin!'

Jade suddenly took off at a gallop, followed by Jemma. Cosy ran after them. She didn't want to get lost! She didn't know the Arcades. She and Mrs Pink had done all their shopping locally, in Grove Park. Because of Mum not being able to get out, Cosy had never really explored anywhere further afield.

'This is *Co*-zee.' Jade flapped a hand at Cosy. 'Short for *Cozy*-mar.'

'She's living with us,' said Jemma.

Dee and Kristin stared at Cosy as if she were some strange blob just dropped by from another planet.

'She goes to the posh school,' said

26

Jade.

'Yeah, an' she talks posh an' all,' said Jemma. She prodded at Cosy. 'Show 'em how you talk! Say something. Go on!'

Cosy pursed her lips.

'She's gone all shy,' said Jade.

'She's a snobby swot,' said Jemma. 'But she knows Darren Walsh's brother. Don't you?' She poked again at Cosy, who nodded. 'He's called Michael Bone.'

'*Bone?*'

'Yeah. Walsh is a stage name, see?'

The four of them moved off, in the direction of the Chocolate Shop. Cosy trailed behind. Jade and Jemma were never going to accept her. She would always be the odd one out. Knowing that she wasn't wanted. Really and truly she would have been far happier staying at home. But she did so want to see Darren Walsh and be able to tell Mum!

There was the hugest crowd of people milling about outside the Chocolate Shop. It was a bit of a disappointment, really. All that happened was that the great Darren Walsh (looking considerably less dishy and considerably more spotty than he did on screen) cut a red ribbon with a pair of scissors and made a little speech about how he loved chocolates, and especially hazelnut clusters, and that was that. A few lucky people at the front managed to get autographs and then he was whisked away, out of sight.

'What a con,' grumbled Kristin.

'Well, at least we got to see him,' said Jade.

Yes, and I can tell Mum that he had a big red spot on his chin! thought Cosy. It wasn't very romantic, having a big red spot on your chin, but it was the sort of thing that would be interesting for Mum to hear. Cosy was saving up lots of these little treasures for when Mum was well enough to have visitors.

'I got to go to the lav,' announced Jemma, suddenly.

'Let's go into Sadler's!'

Sadler's was a big department store. Far bigger than Maplin's, where Cosy and Mrs Pink had bought Cosy's school uniform. It was almost, thought Cosy, the size of a town. As she hurried after the others she wondered how it would be if you got lost and couldn't find your way out. You might have to stay here all night. That would be really spooky.

The four girls, with Cosy tagging on behind, bundled up the escalators to the third floor and crammed their way into the Ladies. There were only four cubicles that didn't have the ENGAGED sign: the four of them went rushing in and slammed the doors. Cosy stood, waiting. She didn't especially want to go to the loo but now that she was here she supposed she might as well. A lady came out at the far end, and Cosy went in. When she came back out again, the others had disappeared.

Cosy stood for a moment, frozen in panic, wondering what to do. They'd gone without her! They'd done it on purpose. Deliberately left her behind!

And then she thought that she was just being silly. They were obviously waiting for her outside.

She rushed out to look.

Nobody!

Maybe that was because they hadn't come out yet?

She rushed back in again. One of the cubicle doors was opening. The one that Jade had gone into. A girl came out, but it wasn't Jade.

Choking back tears of fright and humiliation Cosy ran out of the Ladies' and headed for the escalator, only to discover that the escalator wasn't where she'd remembered it. She'd lost the escalator!

A kind lady took pity on her and pointed her in the right direction. Now all Cosy had to hang on to was the hope that somewhere downstairs the four of them would be waiting for her.

But they weren't. They'd shaken her off because she was a nuisance and a nerd and they hadn't wanted her to go with them in the first place. And now she was on her own! All on her own in a strange part of town. How was she going to get home?

She could ring Guv and ask him to come and collect her. But that would be a *really* feeble thing to do. How could she admit that she was too dumb to find her way back? She wasn't at juniors any more. She was at the high school! She was supposed to have some *brain.*

'Hi, Squit Face!'

Cosy spun round. 'H—hi.'

It was Michael Bone!

'What you doing here? Come to see my brother?'

'Yes.' Cosy said it shyly. She'd never really spoken to Michael. He was older than her, and he'd been one of the popular ones; loud and laughing and up to tricks. Cosy had always been quiet and contained.

'Get his autograph?' said Michael.

Cosy shook her head.

'Want it?'

'Well—' Cosy hesitated. What she really wanted was just to get home!

'I could sell it you.' Michael opened an envelope and pulled out a strip of gummed labels. On every label it said, *Best wishes, Darren Walsh.* 'See? They're genuine!'

'H—how much?' said Cosy.

'Fifty p. Cheap at the price!'

'Could I have two?'

'Have as many as you like.'

'Just two,' said Cosy. One for Jemma, one for Jade. 'And could you tell me where to catch a bus to Dornton Heath?'

Even when Michael had told her she nearly managed to get lost trying to find the bus station. Even when she had found the bus station she nearly wasn't able to find the bus. She understood a bit better now how Mum must feel. Being on your own in a strange place could be rather frightening. It was because she wasn't used to it, of course. People like Michael, like Jade and Jemma, they did it all the time.

' *'Cos they're not nerds*, thought Cosy, miserably.

It was half past twelve when she arrived back at Alma Road. Jade and Jemma hadn't turned up yet.

'All on your own?' said Auntie. 'Where are the others?'

'They . . . had things to do,' said Cosy.

She couldn't confess to Auntie that they had run away and left her. For one thing it would be telling tales, and for another she felt too ashamed. It was horrid being the sort of person that others wanted to run away from!

'They shouldn't have gone off without you,' said Auntie.

'It's all right,' said Cosy. 'I wanted to get back to start on my homework.'

Upstairs in her bedroom she found that she was crying yet again. She did nothing but cry these days. Soon she would have permanently pink eyes. She would look like a rabbit.

Cosy flung herself on to the bed and buried her face in the pillow. *Nerd!* she thought. *Stupid idiotic* nerd.

Somewhere downstairs a door slammed and she heard the sound of voices. Jade and Jemma had obviously arrived back. There was always a lot of shouting and banging when those two were around.

Reluctantly Cosy rolled over on to her back. Now she would have to go down and face them. But at least she had the autographs! They might make them think a bit better of her.

She dragged herself into a sitting

position, scrunching her fists into her eyes. And then stopped, and blinked. Who was that, sitting at her table? No! Not at her table. At a desk. There was a girl, sitting at a desk! A girl with long hair, done into a pigtail. She was holding a pen. She seemed to be writing in some kind of book. Who was she? How had she got there?

Cosy blinked again, and just as suddenly as she had come, the girl was gone. Vanished! Like a puff of smoke.

It made Cosy feel a bit trembly.

I'm going mad, she thought. She had read somewhere that seeing things was one of the first signs of madness. Things that weren't there. But the girl had seemed so real! Another second and Cosy would have opened her mouth and spoken to her.

'Co-zee!' That was Auntie's voice, booming up the stairs. 'Lunch is ready!'

'Coming,' muttered Cosy.

She went slowly down the stairs.

'There you are!' cried Jade.

'What happened to you?' shrieked Jemma.

'We looked all over for you!'

34

'You just disappeared.'

'*Stupid.* I suppose you got lost!'

'You should have taken better care of her,' scolded Auntie.

Jade and Jemma stood shoulder to shoulder, looking at Cosy across the kitchen. Cosy felt that this was some kind of test.

'I expect it was my fault,' she said. At least they would know she wasn't a nerd who told tales. Surely that would make a difference? 'Sometimes I go round with my head in the air.'

'Well, no harm done on this occasion,' said Auntie. 'But don't let it happen again. You two!' She pointed a finger at Jade and Jemma. 'Are you listening? You be a bit more responsible in future.'

Jade stuck out her lower lip in a pout. Jemma looked rebellious.

'I just remembered,' said Cosy, quickly. 'I got you something.' She held out the sticky labels.

'What's this?' said Jemma, ungraciously. 'I can't read it!'

'It says, *Best wishes, Darren Walsh.* It's genuine,' said Cosy.

'Where'd you get it from?'

'I bumped into his brother. He sold them to me.'

She waited for them to say 'Wow' or 'Cor, ta!' or 'Brilliant!'

'Don't really count, coming from his brother,' said Jade.

'Well!' Auntie sent a handful of knives and forks clattering across the table. 'There's gratitude for you!'

'See, it has to come from him himself,' said Jade. 'Not really worth nothing, second-hand.'

'No, I mean, it could be forged,' said Jemma. 'How do we know it isn't forged?'

'Oh, it probably is!' cried Cosy. She snatched back the autographs and stuffed them into the waste bin, among the vegetable peelings and the tea leaves. 'I don't know why I bothered to waste my money!'

There was a silence.

'No. Well.' Jade shrugged a shoulder. 'There you go.'

'We might as well hang on to them,' urged Jemma. She walked across to the bin and delicately, between finger and thumb, picked out the autographs. 'I mean . . . you never know.'

'Talk about having your cake and eating it,' said Auntie.

CHAPTER THREE

'I do miss you ever so much,' sighed Mrs Pink, when Cosy telephoned her on Saturday evening.

'I miss you,' said Cosy, sadly.

'Jonathan misses you, too . . . he keeps going upstairs to look for you.'

'Oh, poor Jonathan!' Just for a moment Cosy almost felt more sorry for Jonathan than she did for herself. At least she *knew* why she had to come and live with strangers. Jonathan only knew that one of his favourite people wasn't there anymore. 'He did so use to love cuddling with me!'

'He will again,' promised Mrs Pink. 'Don't you worry! He won't forget you.'

'But how long can cats remember?' said Cosy.

What she was really trying to say

was, how long do you think it will be before Mum comes out of hospital? Only she was still too scared to ask.

'Oh, cats' memories go on for ever!' said Mrs Pink, cheerfully.

She probably thought it would make Cosy feel better. But if anything it only made her feel worse. Was Mrs Pink saying that it would be for ever before her mum came home?

Cosy took a breath.

'Do you think,' said Cosy, 'that by Christmas—' She stopped.

'I should hope that long before Christmas you'd have come over to visit me!'

'But do you think that Mum—that Mum will be . . .' Cosy's voice faded and dropped away to nothing.

'Well, now,' said Mrs Pink, 'let's keep our fingers crossed, shall we? One thing we know, she's in good hands. She's being well looked after. So you mustn't fret yourself about her! She wouldn't want that, would she?'

Obediently, Cosy shook her head.

'She'd want you to get on with your life and do well at school so she can be proud of you. Because when she comes home she's going to ask you all about it! Isn't that right?'

'Yes,' whispered Cosy.

'And you make sure you keep in touch! You give me a ring now and again. Jonathan's very anxious about you. Aren't you, Jonathan?'

And then Cosy knew that Mrs Pink had turned away and was talking to Jonathan.

'This is Cosy on the phone! Do you want to give her a purr? Go on, give her a purr! Can you hear that, Cosy? That's Jonathan, purring at you. Give him a purr back.'

'Prr, prr,' went Cosy, into the telephone.

Of course, it had to be just then that Jemma came waltzing down the stairs. She stopped and looked at Cosy. Her expression, as plain as anything, said, 'Weedy wet nerd!' Cosy's cheeks fired up. Now she'd be for it.

Sure enough, when Cosy set the telephone down and went to join the others in the sitting-room, Jemma immediately put her hands to her ears and began wiggling her fingers.

'Prr, prr! Was 'oo talking to an ickle pussy, then?'

Cosy blushed, furiously. Blushing was another thing, like crying, that she couldn't seem to stop doing just lately.

'Hey, Pasty Face!' said Jade. Pasty Face was one of her names for her. Pasty Face or Snobby Swot. 'You've gone bright crimson!'

'Looks like she's got the measles,' said Jemma.

'Yeeurgh!' Jade sprang back in mock horror. 'Pasty's got the measles! Keep away from her!'

'What's going on?' Auntie had come bustling into the room. They didn't dare make fun of her when Auntie was there. But Auntie couldn't be there all the time.

'What's happening? What is that television doing on if nobody's watching it?'

'We are watching it!' Jade bounced herself hastily on to the sofa.

'How about Cosy? Is Cosy watching?'

'I'd better not,' said Cosy. 'I've got

homework.'

'On a Saturday evening?' Auntie made a disapproving clicking sound with her tongue. 'That doesn't sound right!'

'It's maths,' said Cosy. Maths always took her ages. 'And some French vocab. and essays.'

She saw Jade and Jemma exchange glances and Jade mouth the words, 'Snobby Swot.'

'They do give you such a lot,' said Auntie. 'Are you sure it isn't too much for you?'

'No!' Cosy backed hurriedly out of the door. She didn't want Auntie complaining to Miss Marriott that she was working too hard or wasn't coping. They might take her scholarship away! Then she would have to go to Hall Cross with Jade and Jemma and Mum would be so disappointed. Cosy would feel she had let her down. 'I can manage! I don't mind!'

'Well, try not to spend all evening,' said Auntie. 'You know what they say . . . all work and no play. Just do half of it and leave the rest for tomorrow.'

'Yeah, 'cos we've got a really good video,' said Jade. '*Axe Murderer.* It's full of blood and heads being chopped off.'

'Just what you like,' said Jemma.

Auntie shook her head. 'Why is it you two are so addicted to horror?'

' 'Cos it's fun!' said Jemma.

'There's this one scene,' gloated Jade, 'where someone's head don't come off first time round so—'

Cosy fled. She knew they hadn't really got a video called *Axe Murderer*; Auntie wouldn't let them. They were just saying it to try to frighten her. They knew she was squeamish about that sort of thing.

There were times when Cosy really envied people like Jade. Jade was always so bold! Always so sure of herself. She might not have won a scholarship to the high school, but nothing ever fazed her. She wasn't squeamish. She didn't blush. It wasn't surprising she and Jemma held Cosy in contempt.

Cosy closed her bedroom door behind her and trailed across the room to sit at her table. Her special homework table. It was true she *did* have a lot of homework, masses and masses of it, but it was also true that she liked to slip away and be by herself. Homework was a good excuse.

All the same, it wasn't a made-up excuse. If you didn't do your homework you were given order marks, and order marks meant trouble. And you couldn't just claim you'd forgotten it because they had all been given special homework books for writing down all the homework that they had to do. Cosy's was already beginning to look quite tattered and torn and she had only been at the school two weeks! But every single teacher seemed to set homework for every single subject. For the weekend she had a whole page of French vocabulary to learn, two pages of maths to get through, and essays to write for English and history.

She didn't mind the essays; she didn't even mind the French vocabulary. It was the maths which paralysed her. Cosy wasn't good at maths. Mum wasn't too good, either, but at least if Mum had been here they could have puzzled it out together. Cosy on her own hardly knew where to begin. She looked at the figures and they simply didn't make any sense. Yet it had all been explained in class! At the time Cosy had thought she understood, but obviously she hadn't. Obviously she was too dim and too stupid.

She arranged the figures one way, then she arranged them another. She crossed them out and she started again. She crossed them out a second time. Then she got in a panic and ripped out the page so that Mrs Adie, the maths teacher, wouldn't be able to see the dreadful mess that she had made.

By eight o'clock, Cosy had shed so many tears that her maths book had great wet splotches all over it. And she still hadn't figured out the answers!

Auntie's voice called up the stairs: 'Cosy! Are you done?'

Cosy ran to the door. 'Nearly!'

'Well, don't stay up there too long. You don't want to be working all night.'

But she hadn't even managed one question! She knew it wasn't any use asking Auntie or Guv to help her. Auntie had already told her, 'I'm afraid you'll be on your own, love, when it comes to homework. I can cook, I can sew, I can garden . . . but I'm not one for the book learning. And the guv'nor, he's the same. He could tell you everything you want to know about the inside of a car. But I don't suppose that's the sort of thing they teach you at that posh school of yours?'

Even Auntie called it the posh school. She didn't say it sneeringly, the way Jade and Jemma did; she was just letting Cosy know that it wasn't her scene. She wasn't one for book learning.

Maybe Cosy wasn't, either. Maybe the scholarship had been a terrible mistake and very soon they would discover that really and truly it should have gone to someone else. That they had muddled up the names and it was some other girl who should be at the high school, not Cosy. Mrs Latymer, the head-mistress, would call Cosy into her office and regretfully inform her that her scholarship was being taken away.

'We are so sorry, Cosy, but you're really not scholarship material. I'm afraid we shall have to let you go.'

How could she ever face Mum if that happened? Cosy flung herself despairingly on to the bed.

'Mum!' she sobbed. 'I can't do it without you! I can't manage on my own!'

She didn't know how long she lay there sobbing but when she had finally sobbed herself to a standstill, because sobbing was exhausting and sooner or later wore you out, she found that the room was quite dark apart from the small circle of light over her homework table. Except—

Cosy struggled into a sitting position. She knuckled at her eyes. It wasn't her homework table! It was the desk. The same desk that she had seen before. With the same girl sitting at it! The girl with the long plait, tied with a piece of ribbon. She was hunched over, writing, with a strange sort of pen that she kept dipping into a little pot that was sunk into a corner of the desk. The pot

46

presumably had ink in it.

Cosy sat, frozen. The girl nibbled the end of her pen, staring up at the darkened window as if wondering what to write. She was wearing a white blouse and a navy blue skirt. And a tie! A stripy tie like boys wore. On her legs she had thick ribbed tights, dark brown, and on her feet, bedroom slippers with little red pom-poms.

She looked strangely old-fashioned. Maybe it was the hair, in its thick chestnut plait. Or maybe it was the skirt. The skirt was so long! And so . . . *lumpy.* No real shape. Cosy wasn't a great one for being in fashion, but even Cosy wouldn't wear a skirt like that!

And then the girl turned, slowly swivelled round on her chair, and looked directly at Cosy. She was frowning, still nibbling at her pen. Cosy shrank back into the shadows. She waited for the girl to say something, but the girl just went on frowning and nibbling. It was as if Cosy could see her, but she couldn't see Cosy.

'She's a ghost!' thought Cosy; and at the realization a shiver ran through her. She was in the same room as a ghost!

Strangely, Cosy didn't feel scared, or in any way threatened. Just a bit . . . shaky. It wasn't every day you found yourself all on your own with a ghost!

But what else could it be?

Experimentally, just in case, Cosy said, 'Hello?' But the girl made no reply. Cosy might never have spoken.

Cosy watched as she turned back to her desk, dipped her pen in the little inkpot, and went on writing. Cosy could hear the scratch of her nib on the paper. She could hear the creak of the chair. And now she could hear something else. An unearthly wailing, like a hooter of some kind. It seemed to be coming from outside. It made all the hairs on Cosy's arms stand up, and prickles go trembling down her spine.

The girl at the desk didn't seem particularly bothered. If anything, she seemed annoyed. She clamped one hand over her ear and went on writing.

A voice called up the stairs.

'Kathleen!' It was a woman's voice, elderly and a bit crackly. 'Come!

Quickly!'

The girl muttered something to herself.

'*Kathleen!*' The voice again, more urgently this time.

'Yes, all right!' The girl threw down her pen. 'Beastly Germans! Beastly bombs! Beastly everything!'

'Kathleen Trimble, I shall not tell you again!'

'Yes, all *right*! I'm *coming*.'

Obviously disgruntled, the girl pushed back her chair and made for the door. Outside, the terrible wailing went on. What could it be? Why had the girl said beastly Germans? Why had she said beastly bombs? Did that mean it was wartime? If so, which war? The one that Mrs Pink liked to talk about?

Mrs Pink had been a young woman in the war. She had shown Cosy photographs of herself wearing a uniform.

'The Wrens,' she said. 'Very smart, we were.'

Other than that, Cosy didn't really know very much about it, except that

49

the British had been fighting the Germans and they had all dropped lots of bombs on each other. She didn't even know when it was except that it was a long time ago. Fifty years? *At least* fifty years, because Mrs Pink had been young and now she was old. The girl with the plait would be old, too, if she was alive now. That was a really spooky thought! Because presumably she couldn't be alive. Not if she was a ghost.

Cosy slid off the bed and tiptoed across the room to where the girl had been sitting. She was scared that if she didn't tread softly the desk and all its contents—the books, the papers, the pen, the inkpot—might vanish the way the girl had vanished earlier on.

But the desk stayed where it was; Cosy managed to creep right up to it. The girl seemed to be keeping some kind of journal; a large book, almost like an account book. She had very neat, sloping handwriting, quite different from the handwriting of people today. Cosy couldn't resist the temptation to take a peek. She knew that journals were supposed to be private, but this one must have been written so long ago!

Myra and Dinky (read Cosy) *said I must have been imagining things. Or dreamt them. Myra said there aren't such things as ghosts. Dinky said that if there were they always carried their head tucked under their arm and dragged a ball and chain, making groaning noises as they came. She said, 'Did yours make groaning noises?' I said no and Dinky said, 'Well, there you are, then!'*

You can't ever talk seriously with Dinky, she turns everything into a joke. And Myra is just too stolid. *I almost begin to wish I hadn't told them. I shan't next time! If it happens again, that is. Which it probably won't, alas!*

Cosy wrinkled her brow. This was odd! Why was the girl talking about ghosts? Had *she* seen one, too? And who were Myra and Dinky? Friends from school, perhaps.

Cosy reached out a hand to turn back a page, so that she could find out, but the most curious thing happened: her hand went right through the book, right through the desk, for all the world as if they weren't there! And now her whole hand was icy cold, really freezing. Cosy tucked her hand into her armpit. Guiltily, her eyes strayed back to the journal.

Tuesday
Had another frightful row with Grandma. Told her I didn't want to go to church any more. Told her I didn't believe in God or the Bible!!! She was really shocked, I think, and I am sorry for that but if there is a God I don't see how He could let this war happen and all the terrible things. Grandma said it is a just war and that Hitler is evil and must be stopped. But what about all the innocent people on BOTH sides that are being killed? Mummy and Daddy, for instance? Why would God, if He exists, punish them and not Hitler?

Grandma says that God moves in mysterious ways and suffering is sent to try us. She says it is not up to us to question, only to do our duty. She says it is my duty to go to church and say my prayers, but I won't! And I have told her so.

I have a feeling that this is just the start of many battles between Grandma and me . . .

Wednesday
I do so hate this horrible war! The siren went early last night and I had to spend ALL NIGHT in the shelter with Gran, who snores like a warthog. She gets on to her back and she won't budge, no matter how hard I kick her. It is so miserable! And I am miserable, too. I miss Mummy and Daddy so much. Sometimes I think the pain is getting worse rather than better. I know I am not alone and that lots of people have lost their loved ones, but it is SO hard to bear. Especially with Gran being so stiff and starchy and unsympathetic!

Thursday
One of the houses in Clyde Road took a terrible battering last night. I think it must have been a direct hit. I saw it as I went to catch the bus for school. The whole of the front has been torn out and you can see right into the rooms. In one I

saw a child's doll hanging half over the edge, with an arm dangling into space. It looked so pathetic! And I couldn't help wondering what had happened to the child who owned it. I don't know who lived there but Grandma would probably be able to tell me. However, I can't ask her, as she is still being decidedly frosty towards me. In any case, I am not sure that I really want to know. It makes me think of Mummy and Daddy. And that makes me too sad.

Friday
I have just seen her again! The ghost girl. I am DEFINITELY not imagining it. She was really here! In the room! I don't believe that she is able to see ME, at least she gives no sign of doing so, but I saw her as clear as day! And I wasn't asleep so I can't have been dreaming. We'd just had tea and I came racing upstairs to make an entry in my journal, and there she was, sitting at her table and looking most dreadfully unhappy. Almost as unhappy as I quite often feel. In her case it is something to do with homework, I think. Some maths that she cannot

understand.

Maths? thought Cosy. This was becoming seriously weird. She read on, with a growing sense of wonderment.

It is very simple maths, the sort we did in the Lower III. But maybe that is the form the ghost girl is. She is younger than I am; I should say about ten or eleven. I don't know why she finds it so difficult but I must remember that not everyone enjoys maths the way I do. But we can't all be good at everything and the essay she wrote the other day for English got an A–. I saw it in her English book!

Cosy was growing more and more bewildered. It was perfectly true that Mrs Kemp had given her an A–.

'Excellent work, Cosy! Very nicely written.'

But how had this girl seen it? She was a ghost!

I am really very puzzled, wrote Kathleen, *as to where this strange little creature can be from. From the past, obviously; but she wears such strange clothes! Leggings in bright colours—today they were red, with a pattern of yellow zigzags. Almost like a boy from*

Elizabethan times. But she is not a boy! And on her top half she wears a sort of VEST, with sleeves. Maybe it is what she wears for bed? Instead of a nightdress? I am racking my brains for any period of history where girls dressed in such a curious way.

I have racked them! Racked and racked, and I can't think of a single one. Maybe it was some strange fashion in Grandma's youth and she would know about it. It can't have been from too far back or she would not be doing maths or writing with a fountain pen. At least, I suppose it is a fountain pen, as she does not have to keep dipping it, but it is not like any fountain pen that I have seen.

Ballpoint, thought Cosy. Maybe they didn't have them in the war?

I am so excited at seeing my ghost girl! Wherever she has come from, it is like an echo across time. I feel that

And there the sentence stopped. Chopped off short. Cosy discovered why as she read on.

Bother! Bother and blast and drat! There goes the siren. AGAIN. That is two nights running. Wouldn't you think they could give us a rest?

Now Grandma is yelling up the stairs. She gets in such a flap if we don't rush to the shelter immediately.

Yes, all right! I am coming.

That will be another night with the warthog. I shall occupy myself by thinking of my strange little ghost girl in her red leggings and vest. I wish I knew more about her! Especially which part of history she comes from. I must ask Gran if the house is haunted.

Well! Cosy, in her red leggings and T-shirt, turned to look at herself in the mirror. Her reflection stared back, lank-haired and pudding-faced, just the same as always. How could *she* be a ghost girl? Kathleen was the ghost! She was the one who came from the past, not Cosy.

On sudden impulse, Cosy ran to the door. Carefully she eased it open, expecting—she wasn't sure what. But there was the landing, there were the stairs; there was the sound of the television, blaring from the front room. No different from usual. And Auntie's voice, calling to her: 'Cosy! Haven't you finished yet?'

She would have to go down. Cosy turned back for one last quick glance into her bedroom. The desk had gone! In its place was Cosy's table, with her school books and her dreaded maths homework. Still not finished. But as Kathleen had said, you couldn't be good at everything. And she had got an A– for her essay.

Cosy closed the door behind her and ran lightly down the stairs. She had had enough of maths homework for one night!

CHAPTER FOUR

All night long Cosy dreamt about the ghost girl . . . Kathleen. Kathleen Trimble. Trimble was a funny kind of name, but then everybody seemed to consider Cosy's name rather odd.

Kathleen Trimble thought Cosy was a ghost! *But how can I be?* thought Cosy. *I am in the* future. How could you have a ghost that came from your future? Ghosts came from the past! They were people who had died young or who had been killed in tragic circumstances. People with unfinished business, who haunted the earth in ghostly form.

It was really spooky! Yet Kathleen wasn't spooky. And it was hard to believe that she was dead. She had looked so alive, sitting there at her desk. Just as alive as Cosy had obviously looked to her.

But I am *alive!* thought Cosy. What a puzzle it was! But exciting, as well. If anyone had told Cosy, this time yesterday, that she would be lying in bed in a room that was haunted, she never would have believed them. Cosy was scared of ghosts! Yet she wasn't in the least bit scared of Kathleen. It was almost like having a special and particular friend that no one else knew about.

And I am going to keep it that way, vowed Cosy. The ghost girl was *Cosy's* friend. She didn't want Jade and Jemma bursting in and taking over, which was exactly what they would do.

All the same, at breakfast next morning she couldn't help asking Auntie if she knew anything about the history of the house.

'About the people that lived here?'

'I'm afraid I don't,' said Auntie. 'Me and Guv, we've been here ten years. We got it cheap, off the Council. They were going to widen the road but they never got around to it, so me and Guv fell in lucky.'

If Mum and Cosy had lived in an old house they would never have rested till they had unearthed its past and learnt about all the families that had lived there, but Auntie wasn't like Mum. She wasn't interested in days gone by. Auntie was very much a person of the present.

'The past is gone and the future can look after itself,' was Auntie's way of thinking.

It was a bit disappointing but Cosy thought perhaps you couldn't have everything. Auntie could cook and sew and grow things in the garden. She could look after nerdy people like Cosy and tearaways like Jade and Jemma.

You couldn't expect her to take an interest in people from the past as well.

'What d'you wanna know for, anyway?' said Jade.

'Only 'cos it's an old house,' said Cosy. She reached out a hand for the milk jug. 'I thought it might be haunted.'

'What a thing to suggest!' scolded Auntie. 'Of course it isn't haunted! You can forget that idea straight away, my girl! We don't want you giving yourself nightmares.'

'I wouldn't have nightmares,' said Cosy. 'I'd quite like to see a ghost.'

'Well, you won't be seeing one in this house,' said Auntie.

'Bet if she did she'd scream the place down,' said Jemma.

'Now you just listen to me! I shall only say it once,' said Auntie. *There are no ghosts at 44 Alma Road.*'

'How do we *know*?' said Jemma. 'Could be dead headless bodies moaning all over the place. It's just we haven't seen 'em.'

'No! Because there's nothing *to* see. You just stop putting ideas into her head. It's all right, Cosy, love!' Auntie leant across the table to pat Cosy's hand. 'You can get on with your breakfast and don't worry about it.'

I'm not worried, thought Cosy. Auntie was the one that was worried. That was because she thought Cosy was afraid. But she wasn't! She had seen a ghost and it hadn't frightened her *one little bit.*

Cosy hugged her secret to herself. She would have liked someone to share it with, but she hadn't yet made any friends at the high school, not real friends, and she never saw any of the people she had known at Juniors. They all lived on the other side of town. That only left Jemma and Jade, and she didn't think they would ever want to be friends with her. She was too much of a snobby swot and she wasn't any fun. Cosy meekly accepted it. The person she felt closest to was the Ghost Girl.

The Ghost Girl was unhappy, just like Cosy. She'd lost her mum and dad, and her gran obviously didn't understand her. Cosy wished she would come back and write some more in her journal. She looked for her every evening when she sat down to do her homework, every night when she climbed into bed. Sometimes she even woke up in the early hours in the hope of seeing her, but she never did.

*   *   *

On Friday, Mrs Adie gave Year 7 their maths homework back. Cosy's was covered all over in red ink. At the bottom Mrs Adie had written, 'Please stay behind and see me at the end of the lesson.'

'Well, Cosy!' Mrs Adie sounded more hurt than angry. As if she couldn't believe that anyone could do this to her. 'What went wrong?'

Cosy shuffled, uncomfortably. 'Don't know, miss.'

'Mrs Adie.'

They didn't like you calling them 'miss' at the high school. You had to call them by their names. Cosy didn't always remember.

'I do expect better,' said Mrs Adie, 'from someone like you.'

63

She meant someone who was on a scholarship. People on scholarships were supposed to be brainy. It was being there under false pretences, otherwise. Cosy felt almost as if Mrs Adie were accusing her of cheating. Taking scholarship money and then not being able to do simple maths!

'We went through it all in class,' said Mrs Adie. 'Did you not understand it?'

'I did at the time,' mumbled Cosy.

'You mean . . . it just went out of your head?'

Cosy twizzled a length of hair round her finger.

'Cosy, if you don't properly understand something,' said Mrs Adie, 'you must put up your hand and ask. Don't just sit there and say nothing! How about today? Have you understood what we did today?'

'Mm . . .' Cosy nodded, uncertainly. Today had been algebra. Lots of little letters—$a+b^2$ and things in brackets. She was hoping that letters might make a bit more sense than numbers.

'Well, see how you get on. Just sit down to it, calmly, and try to be logical.

It's all common sense, you know! There's nothing magic about it.'

That afternoon, as soon as tea was over, Cosy rushed upstairs to her desk. She had to solve the riddle of all those little letters before the magic escaped her!

It *was* magic. It had to be! She didn't care what Mrs Adie said. It was like people pulling rabbits out of hats. You either knew how to do it or you didn't. It wasn't something you could work out for yourself like 'What is this poem saying?' or 'What does the author mean by this?'

Cosy gazed despairingly at a row of letters. Already a familiar sense of panic was setting in. What were you supposed to do with them? All those letters! They didn't make any more sense than numbers!

$6a + 2b - 3a + 1$, wrote Cosy.

Her hand began to shake. Moths fluttered in her stomach. *Mum, I can't do this! I need you, Mum!*

'Co-zee!' Auntie's voice came bellowing up the stairs. 'Miss Marriott's here to see you!'

65

Cosy set down her pen. Her hand was trembling, and her legs, as she pushed away from the desk, felt weak and wobbly. This would be the second week she hadn't been able to do her maths homework! Mrs Adie was going to be furious!

I told you, Cosy, if you didn't properly understand something . . .

But if you were on a scholarship you were supposed to understand! It was like cheating if you didn't.

'Co-zee! Did you hear me?'

Cosy pushed some limp strands of hair behind her ears and went out on to the landing.

'Yes, I'm coming.'

As Cosy was on her way down, Jade came galumphing up. She hissed, 'Your minder's here! Come to check if you've been behaving yourself.'

Miss Marriott was waiting for Cosy in the front room.

'Hello, Cosy! How are things?'

'All right,' whispered Cosy.

'No problems?'

Cosy shook her head.

'The other two giving you any

hassle?'

'N—no,' said Cosy. 'N—not really.'

'They can be a bit overpowering. You mustn't let them push you around. Just because they were here first doesn't mean they have any more claim on the Ridleys' attention than you do. How do you get on with the Ridleys?'

'They're nice,' said Cosy.

'They are, aren't they? I knew you'd be happy with them. Everybody loves Auntie and Guv! What about your schoolwork? How's that going?'

'OK,' said Cosy.

'Are you managing to keep up?'

Cosy nodded, dismally. There didn't seem much point telling Miss Marriott that she couldn't do her maths. She would get to hear about it soon enough, when they took her scholarship away.

'Good!' said Miss Marriott. 'I'm glad. You've had such a shaky start. Now! About your mum.'

Cosy's heart, which had slowed to a dull thud, immediately picked up and began racing. Mum! Was she going to come home?

'I spoke to the hospital,' said Miss Marriott. 'I thought it would be nice if we could arrange a visit for you. But they feel it would be better if we left it for a while. Next month, maybe. We'll try again then, shall we? See how she's doing. In the meantime, you keep up the good work at school, so you'll be able to tell her about it!'

Miss Marriott went breezing out. She seemed pleased with herself, as if she had brought Cosy good news. Next month, *maybe*, *Cosy* could see her mum.

The tears stung Cosy's eyes. Did Mum know that she was having to live with strangers? Did Mum ever think about her? Or was she lost in another world, where Cosy was nothing but a blurred shadow-figure that no longer meant anything?

'Hey!' The door had slammed open and Jade and Jemma had come bundling in. 'Naff off, swot features! Time for telly!'

'Naff off yourself!' cried Cosy.

Jade's mouth dropped open. Jemma giggled.

'Well, get *her*,' said Jade.

'Stupid carrot top!' screeched Cosy.

She pounded up the stairs, heart beating furiously, tears spurting from her eyes. She hated them! She hated them! She would never be friends with them, not even if they begged her!

Cosy stumbled into her bedroom, half blinded by tears. She blundered across to her desk—and then stopped, with a gasp. The Ghost Girl was back! Sitting there, writing.

Holding her breath, Cosy stole closer. She was so close, now, that she could reach out a hand and—

The girl turned. Hastily, Cosy pulled her hand back. Who knew what might happen if you tried touching a ghost?

For a few seconds the girl sat there, head to one side, as if listening for a sound that she was not quite sure of. Cosy remained where she was, frozen into stillness. The girl shook her head, obviously puzzled, and went back to her writing. Cosy watched, over her shoulder, as she formed the words.

I have just had the most eerie sensation! I could have sworn, just for a moment, that there was someone standing behind me. But there is no one there and so I suppose I must have been imagining it. I thought perhaps my little sad ghost person had come back. For she was here, just a while ago! I saw her as clearly as I can see myself in the mirror.

She was seated at her table, weeping once again over her maths homework. Algebra, today. And really such simple stuff! I wish there was some way I could help her. I hate to see her so despairing! She is a dear little thing, with such a sweet little round face, all pink and puckered with the tears she sheds.

Dear little thing? thought Cosy. No one had called her a dear little thing before!

Her clothes were a bit more normal today—a blouse and skirt, almost like school uniform. Almost like my *school uniform, except that she has no tie and her skirt barely reaches her knees! I think Miss Fothergill would have a fit if I went to school with my skirt above my knees!!!*

I remember seeing pictures of Mum wearing short skirts. That was before I was born. Nineteen twenty-something.

But even Mum's skirts didn't come above her knees! And I am sure they never wore bright coloured leggings. I asked Grandma the other day if she had ever worn leggings, all by themselves with just a vest, and she froze like an icicle and said, 'Certainly not! We dressed for modesty in my day.' And then she wanted to know wherever I could have got such a notion from. I couldn't think what to tell her but fortunately she answered herself—with a disapproving sniff! 'From America, I suppose.' Everything bad comes from America!

So I am no closer to solving this very strange mystery. All I know is that I have become incredibly fond of my little ghosty person and would give anything to . . .

'Hey! Teacosy!'

Cosy sprang round. Jade and Jemma were at the door, beating on it like a couple of battering rams.

'You in there?'

What a nuisance they were!

'Teacosy?'

'Yes,' said Cosy. 'What do you want?'

'OK we come in?'

Cosy was about to shout 'No!' but

too late. They were already cramming themselves through the door—and the Ghost Girl had gone.

'What is it?' said Cosy.

Really, these girls had no manners at all.

'Gave up on the telly,' said Jade. 'Load of rubbish. Wanna come an' play Catwalk?'

'What's Catwalk?'

'It's this game we've got.' Jemma bounced down on to Cosy's bed. 'What we do, we put on make-up and do our hair different and get dressed up and stuff and pretend to be models.'

Cosy put a finger in her mouth and tore at a flap of skin.

'I haven't got any make-up.'

She waited for them to sneer and say, 'No, well, you wouldn't have, would you?' Instead, Jade just grinned and assured her that she and Jemma had 'loads'.

'We don't mind you using it,' said Jemma.

'Yeah, 'cos it's more fun with three.'

Cosy hesitated. 'What about my maths homework?'

'Forget about your homework!'

'Get cool!'

Well, thought Cosy, what did homework matter? They could only take her scholarship away. Then she'd go to school with Jade and Jemma. It mightn't be so bad. At least they wouldn't call her snobby swot any more.

'C'mon!' Jade tugged at her.

Cosy allowed herself to be shepherded along the passage to the room that the two of them shared. She had never been in there before. It was large and airy with a curtain down the middle.

'Auntie made the curtain,' said Jade. 'She did it so's we could be private.'

'If we wanted,' said Jemma.

'Well, yeah. If we wanted. We don't usually, do we?'

'Not usually.'

'Before you come,' said Jade, 'we had our own rooms. I had your one.'

'Oh!' Cosy felt herself blushing. How awful! She had taken Jade's room. No wonder they resented her. 'I didn't realize.'

' 'S all right,' said Jade. 'We don't mind. Look! This is our make-up.'

She pulled a large cardboard box from under one of the beds and sent the contents spilling across the duvet. Cosy gaped.

'Where'd you get all that from?'

Jade tapped a finger to the side of her nose. 'Them as asks no questions . . .'

'We just kind of . . . pick it up,' said Jemma. 'As we go round. Know what I mean?'

Cosy swallowed. 'Yes, I—I think so.'

'You gonna tell on us?'

'No! I didn't tell before,' said Cosy.

'What d'you mean, you didn't tell before?'

'L-last Saturday,' stammered Cosy. 'When we went to see Darren Walsh.'

'Oh! Yeah. Right.'

'Just as well,' said Jade. 'We'd have bashed you, else!'

Cosy stayed in Jade and Jemma's room playing Catwalk all the rest of the evening. They painted their eyes and lip-glossed their lips and gave themselves huge spiky eyelashes that looked like spiders' legs. They combed their hair into weird and wonderful shapes and used a pair of Auntie's high heels to totter about on. Jade and Jemma had bikini tops which they stuffed with rolled-up tights to look like bosoms.

Across the room they had balanced a long plank of wood on piles of books: this was the catwalk. One pile of books was higher than the other so that the plank sloped quite sharply. The idea was to walk up and down it without giggling so much that they fell off. Towards the end they all did rather a lot of falling off.

'See?' said Jemma. 'It's fun, innit?'

'Yeah!' Cosy was doing her best to try to talk more like Jade and Jemma and less like a stuffy high school girl. After all, where had talking nicely got Mum? In hospital. Shut away from the world. From now on, Cosy was going to be like everyone else. Bother home-work! Bother talking nicely! Bother scholarships! What did she care?

'Wanna do it again some time?' said Jade.

'Yeah!' Cosy gave a little swagger. 'Why not?'

She didn't do any of her maths homework. And for the first time since coming to Alma Road she went to sleep without saying good night to Mum . . .

CHAPTER FIVE

'Forgot?' said Mrs Adie. She drew herself up, very stiff and straight. 'You *forgot*?'

'Yeah,' said Cosy. 'I'm sorry,' she added.

'Sorry isn't good enough, and please don't say *yeah*. The word is *yes*. What do you mean, you forgot? Did you not put it in your homework book?'

'Yea-yes. But I—I forgot!'

Mrs Adie breathed, rather heavily. She stood, looking down at Cosy from what seemed a great height. Cosy stared back, unblinking.

'Cosy, this is not like you,' said Mrs Adie.

No, it wasn't! This was the new Cosy. Cosy the Bold. Cosy the Fearless. Cosy who didn't give a rap!

'You'd better take an order mark,' said Mrs Adie. 'And just make sure it doesn't occur again!'

Mrs Adie wasn't the first person to have given Cosy an order mark that week. Mr McEvoy, the RE teacher, had given her one for running in the corridor. You weren't supposed to run in corridors. Not at the stuffy old High School for Girls.

A *stupid* rule, thought Cosy. Stupid rule for a stupid school!

She had also been in trouble with Miss Addison, her form mistress, for using bad language. A girl called Michelle Morgan, who had long blonde hair and rather fancied herself, had been fixing a notice on the form notice board with a drawing pin. The drawing pin had fallen down and rolled beneath a desk. Seeing Cosy nearby, Michelle had said, 'Just get that up, will you?' Normally Cosy wouldn't have hesitated to obey an order from the great Michelle Morgan. But this was the new

Cosy! Cosy-the-worm-who-had-turned.

'*Please,*' said Cosy.

'Look, just get it up!' said Michelle.

'Shan't,' said Cosy.

'Well!' Michelle put her hands on her hips. 'What an extremely unpleasant little person you are.'

'Oh, go boil yourself!' yelled Cosy. 'Stupid naffing twot!'

She didn't actually know what a stupid naffing twot was, but it sounded dead right for Michelle. It was something she had picked up from Jade and Jemma. Unfortunately, Miss Addison came into the room just in time to hear it.

'Cosy Walker!' she said. 'Do my ears deceive me? We won't have any of that kind of gutter language in *my* classroom, thank you very much.'

And then, oh heavens, even gentle little Miss Rosen, who took them for art, had a go at her. It wasn't even Cosy's fault. It was that big pushy Pandora. Pandora Rivers-Smith. Ugh! She'd tried to swipe Cosy's seat, just because it was next to Chloe Rowlands, and everyone wanted to sit next to

Chloe. Well, Cosy didn't especially, but it was *her* seat, she'd bagged it first.

Pandora was really gobsmacked when Cosy wouldn't let her have it. They were all used to Cosy being a doormat.

'Look, just shove over!' said Pandora; and she gave Cosy a push.

'I was here first,' said Cosy.

'So what? It's my seat, usually.'

'Well, it's not today,' said Cosy. 'It's mine. So naff off!'

'Cosy!' Miss Rosen sounded shocked. 'What did I hear you say?'

'Naff off,' said Cosy.

Somebody giggled. It might have been Chloe.

'That's not very nice,' said Miss Rosen, 'is it?'

'Wasn't meant to be,' muttered Cosy.

If she had only said sorry, Miss Rosen would have forgotten all about it. Miss Rosen didn't like getting people into trouble. But Cosy wasn't sorry and had no intention of saying that she was.

'I can't believe you meant it,' prompted Miss Rosen.

79

'Well, I did,' said Cosy.

Chloe giggled again and clamped a hand to her mouth. And Miss Rosen reported Cosy to Miss Addison and Miss Addison called Cosy in for a serious talk.

'I can't understand what's come over you, Cosy! I hear nothing but complaints about you. You seem to have developed an attitude problem. What's behind it all? Is it to do with your mum?'

Cosy pursed her lips. She didn't want to talk about her mum.

'Is she still in the hospital?'

'Mm.' Cosy nodded.

'Are you able to go and visit her?'

Cosy shook her head.

'Are you worried about her?'

'Nope.' Cosy pushed her hair back behind her ears.

'You're not?'

'Nope.'

'Are you quite sure?'

'She's been in hospital before,' said Cosy. 'I'm used to it.'

'Well. All right, if you say so.' Miss Addison looked at Cosy. She seemed at a loss. 'Is it the work? Are you finding the work too much for you?'

Cosy humped a shoulder. 'Not 'specially.' Only maths. The rest was all right.

'If you are, you know,' said Miss Addison, "you must come to me and say so. That's what I'm here for, to help. We never mind if someone admits to having honest difficulties. But what we will not tolerate—' here, a touch of frost entered Miss Addison's voice—'is sheer bad manners. There is simply no excuse for that kind of thing, and I am warning you, Cosy, if there is any more of it you are going to find yourself in trouble. You've been given a great opportunity, you know. It's not many people who qualify for a scholarship. Don't waste it! If you won't think of yourself, then think of your mum. I bet she's really proud of you, isn't she?'

Cosy remained stubbornly silent.

'Think how you'd be letting her down,' urged Miss Addison. 'She'd be so disappointed!'

So what? Cosy biffed angrily with her

schoolbag against a row of iron railings as she walked to the bus stop that afternoon. She didn't care about Mum! Mum was the one who had let Cosy down. Running back to hospital just when Cosy needed her most. Being cosseted and cared for while Cosy had to live with strangers and be jeered at for talking posh and for being a stupid snobby swot. It wasn't fair! It just wasn't *fair*!

Her homework book was full of all the homework she had to do—ghastly geography, foul physics, hateful, horrible, *loathsome* maths—but instead of going upstairs to sit at her table she went to knock on Jade and Jemma's door.

'What d'you want, Teacosy?'

'Are we going—gonna—play Catwalk again?' said Cosy.

'Might be,' said Jemma. 'Why?'

' 'Cos I enjoyed it.'

'But it's a weekday,' said Jade.

'So what?' Cosy gave another of the little swaggers she had been educating. Jade walked with a swagger and Cosy was determined to do the same.

82

'You got your homework,' said Jemma.

'Pish to homework!'

They studied her, curiously. She felt like a specimen in a specimen jar.

'What's got into you?' said Jade. 'What about your swotting?'

'Not gonna do it no more.'

'Why not?'

'Don't wanna. ' 'S waste o' time.'

'You'll get into a row,' said Jemma.

'I don't give a pig's bum!' shrieked Cosy.

Jemma giggled. 'She's getting to sound almost human!'

Cosy strutted. 'So? We gonna play?'

'*No.*' Jade suddenly stepped forward. 'This ain't right,' she said.

'Why ain't it?' said Cosy.

' 'Cos it ain't! You got a scholarship, you ought to work real hard.'

'I *bin* working real hard! I'm sick of it! I wanna have fun! I wanna play Catwalk! I wanna—'

'I don't care what you bleedin' well want.' Jade pushed Cosy back out on to the landing. 'It ain't a question of what you want.'

83

'Yes, it is! It's my life. I can do what I like with my life!'

'Not while I'm around,' said Jade.

'Let me go! Stop yanking me!'

Cosy struggled, but Jade was too strong. With one hand gripping the back of Cosy's collar and the other hand under her elbow, she frogmarched Cosy down the passage to her own room.

'You just get in there and do your homework!'

'No! I won't! I don't wanna!'

'Well, you gotta!' Jade opened the door and booted Cosy through it. 'We'll play again at the weekend. And just stop *talkin'* like that. It ain't nat'ral!'

Cosy stumbled across the room. She picked up her maths book and hurled it as hard as she could against the wall. Then she screamed out all the bad words she could think of.

'Pig's bum God's-teeth rot-in-HELL damn-and-blast and blimey naffing scumbag PISSPOT!'

And then she saw Mum's photograph, which her maths book had

knocked to the floor. She bent to pick it up and found that the glass had cracked so that Mum's face had splinters all over it.

'Mum!'

Now Cosy couldn't even kiss her. She *hadn't* kissed her for days. She had been too angry.

'Mum, I didn't mean it,' she whispered.

She had wanted to take her revenge on Mum. Mum had deserted her! It would serve her right if Cosy's scholarship was taken away. Then Cosy could go to Mum and shout, 'See? This is what comes of you leaving me!' As if Mum had done it on purpose. As if she could help being ill!

Very carefully, Cosy pressed her lips to the cracked glass. On Saturday she would buy Mum a new frame. She set the photograph back on her bedside table. Then she picked up her maths book. She couldn't be unkind to Mum! She would do her maths homework if it took her all night. She would do what Mrs Adie had said. She would be calm and use her common sense. After all, she had managed maths OK when she was at Juniors. That had only been a few short months ago. It couldn't be all that different.

Oh, but it was! It was the little letters again, and the brackets, and the numbers stuck up in the air.

Find the numerical values of the following, said Exercise Number 1 in Cosy's homework book.

$a^2b \times ab^2$ *when a = 1, b = 2*

Cosy's heart began to thud and hammer. Her hand shook, her stomach clenched.

Keep calm! *Calm!* Use your common sense.

Right—a^2 meant $a \times a$, she knew that much. And $a = 1$, so that made it 1×1.

But what were you supposed to do with b? Add it to a? Or did you multiply? Or even divide?

And what did ab^2 mean? She didn't know what it meant! She didn't know what to do with it! $a = 1$ and $b = 2$, so was it $1 + 2$ or 1×2 or 1 *divided* by two—

What was 1 divided by 2?

'*Oh!*' Cosy threw down her pen. She rushed over to the wall and began beating her head frantically against it. It's no—*use*! I can't *do* it! It's no *use*! I can't *do* it!

She beat and beat until her head was ringing, then exhausted she slid to the floor and lay there, in a heap, weeping helplessly. A voice called, from downstairs:

'Kathleen! Are you in bed yet?'

'Nearly, Grandma!'

Cosy's head jerked up. The Ghost Girl! The Ghost Girl was here! At her desk, the same as always. Only this time, instead of her school skirt and blouse she was wearing a pink woolly dressing gown with the hem of a pink nightie showing beneath it. On her feet were her slippers with the pom-poms.

The voice called again: 'It's time to put that light out!'

'*Yes*, Grandma.'

The Ghost Girl pulled a face. She laid down her pen and walked across the floor. The door opened, and closed behind her. She must be going to the bathroom, thought Cosy. Greatly daring, Cosy crept across the room to the Ghost Girl's desk. She had been writing in her journal, as usual. She had been writing about Cosy!

I miss her when she is not here (read Cosy). *My funny little ghosty person. I haven't seen her for simply ages. Weeks and weeks!*

But I have seen her, thought Cosy. Cosy had seen the Ghost Girl only last Saturday. Did that mean that time *there* was different from time *here*?

I do hope she has not deserted me! I like to feel that she is close, that we are somehow sharing the same space. I wish she would come back! She might take my mind off things.

By 'things', of course, I mean my battles with Grandma. She can be so hateful at times! She doesn't understand me at all. She doesn't even try. She is IMPLACABLY opposed to my going to medical school. She says it would be a ridiculous waste of money, as I would be bound to get married and start having babies before I was even halfway through the course.

I assured her that I would NOT. I said

that if she liked I would even swear on the Bible, but she didn't care for that suggestion. Seemed to think it was blasphemy on my part, me having said I didn't believe in the Bible, etc. She says if I am interested in medicine I can always train to be a nurse. She has no objection to girls being nurses. That is a proper FEMININE thing to be.

Honestly, she is so old-fashioned it is unbelievable! She makes NO attempt to move with the times. But I am going to be a doctor, come what may! I will fight her every inch of the way. I am UTTERLY DETERMINED.

Oh, if Mum and Dad were only here! They would have encouraged me, I am sure they would. As it is I am having to do it all by myself, for Grandma and I are at daggers drawn. She said to me today, 'I don't care for your attitude, Kathleen.' Well! I don't care for hers, either. She is old and crotchety and thoroughly selfish. And I am miserable, miserable, MISERABLE.

The strangest thing! I have just been downstairs to fetch my bedtime milk, which Grandma insists that I have even though I have told her not once but a million times that I hate it and that hot milk makes me feel sick, and lo and behold when I came back upstairs my darling little ghosty person was here!

The poor little thing is in a state once again about her maths. She has made SUCH a mess! And all of it is wrong. She obviously has no head for figures. It would help if she didn't panic so. Panic is no use! It squeezes all the sense out of one's brain. In the end she went to beat her head against the wall, she was in such despair. I wish there was some way I could help her!

If I could just sit down with her and take her through it, step by step, she would see how easy it really is. But I am almost sure that she cannot see me. And now she is gone again—just slipped away even as I watched.

Where does she go? Where does she come from? I would so love to know!

Grandma has just yelled at me to put the light out. Dinky is allowed to stay up as late as she likes, till 11 o'clock sometimes. Why does Grandma have to treat me like a child? I am not a child! I am almost fifteen!

Cosy came to the end of the page. So the Ghost Girl had seen the mess that she had made in her maths book. And all of it wrong! Cosy had known it was wrong. The tears came back to her eyes and she blinked them away, furiously. The Ghost Girl must think she did nothing but cry!

The door opened again. She had come back! The Ghost Girl had come back! Cosy held her breath as she walked across the room. She was supposed to be going to bed, her grandmother had told her it was time to turn the light out, but instead she was sitting down once more at her desk. She was picking up her pen, dipping it in the ink pot.

Cosy watched as she wrote.

It really bothers me that I can do nothing to help my poor little ghost in her distress. It is so frustrating! If I could only say to her, 'See! This is how it is done.' And then I would write out a sum—for instance, $a^2b^2 \times ab^2$—and we would go through it together, so slowly, so carefully! I would make it really

91

simple for her. Like this:

a^2b^2 x ab^2 can also be written as follows—a × a × b × b × a × b × b

Thus, if a = 2 and b = 3, we have—2×2 × 3×3 × 2×3×3

That is what I would do! And then she would understand, and could apply the principle to all the rest of her exercises.

But, alas, she is a ghost and there can be no way of communicating with her.

Cosy stood staring at the Ghost Girl's figures. Slowly, as she stared, they began to make sense.

'I *see*!' said Cosy.

The Ghost Girl laid down her pen. With a sigh, she went over to the bed, climbed beneath the covers and switched off the light. For a few seconds the room was in darkness; and when the darkness cleared the Ghost Girl had gone. So had her figures! But Cosy had seen, and had understood. The Ghost Girl had laid it out so clearly!

Quickly, quickly, before it could go from her again, Cosy snatched up her pen.

a^2b × ab^2 = a × a × b × a × b × b

She knew how to do it! At last! She wasn't as stupid as she'd thought she was!

CHAPTER SIX

On Saturday, at breakfast, Guv said, 'Anyone want to earn themselves a bit of extra pocket money?'

Jade and Jemma exchanged glances.

'Depends,' said Jade.

'All right! Let's put it another way. Anyone out of the kindness of their heart want to help a poor old man clear out his cellar?'

'What poor old man?' said Jemma.

'This one,' said Guv. He stabbed a finger at himself. 'This poor old man sitting right here.'

'You're not as old as all that,' said Cosy, kindly.

'Old enough,' said Guv. 'Old enough. I could do with some young legs to run up and down those stairs for me.'

'I'll run up and down them for you,'

93

said Cosy.

'What about you two? Feel like lending a hand? I don't reckon little Tea Cosy here could manage on her own.'

'No, she is a bit of a weed,' agreed Jade. She didn't say it nastily, as once she would have done. She was just, like . . . pulling Cosy's leg. Cosy didn't mind any more. It was friendly; it didn't bother her.

'So how about it?' said Guv.

'Why does the cellar *need* clearing out?' said Jemma.

'Well, now.' Guv looked at Auntie and winked. 'That *was* going to be our little secret, but since you ask . . . we'd thought of turning it into a den for you girls.'

'Oh.' Jemma's mouth dropped open.

'It means you could play your music down there,' said Auntie, 'without annoying anyone. And have your friends round and lounge about and do whatever it is you do.'

'But first,' said Guv, 'there's generations of clutter that has to be got rid of.'

'In that case—' Impulsively, Jade pushed back her chair, raced round the table and caught Guv's neck in a stranglehold. 'Mwah!' went Jade, planting a big smacker of a kiss on Guv's leathery cheek. 'In that case, we'll do it for free! Won't we?' She glared at Jemma, daring her to contradict. 'Do it for free? Right?'

'Yeah! Right.' Jemma nodded.

'Absolutely,' said Cosy.

Cosy would have done it anyway. She loved the idea of grubbing about in the cellar. Auntie didn't normally let them go down there; she said it was too dirty.

All morning long the three girls raced up and down the creaking wooden steps carting old broken chairs and television sets, ancient car parts, battered paint pots, lengths of wood which Guv thought he might like to keep ('Could come in handy.' 'Nonsense! Chuck it all away!' said Auntie), bits of rusting metal, an ironing board that was falling to pieces, a lawnmower without any blades, pots and pans and piles of old newspapers (which Cosy wanted to stop and read but 'We haven't got time!' urged Jade).

Everything had to be carried out through the kitchen, into the garden and round the side of the house to a waiting skip. Jade and Jemma threw things in from a distance, over the garden gate, because they liked the loud clanging noise they made. When Cosy tried it she missed the skip and almost hit a passer-by, which Jade and Jemma thought hilarious.

'You have a very peculiar sense of humour,' Cosy told them, crossly. She could say things like that these days. She was quite often bold. 'I might have killed her!'

Jade screeched and Jemma clutched her stomach.

'Killed by a flying bucket!'

'It's not funny,' said Cosy.

'It is,' yelped Jade. 'It's hysterical!'

'It's what's known as black comedy,' said Jemma.

'*Sick* comedy, more like,' muttered Cosy.

The cellar was nearly empty; there were just a few odd items of furniture to be cleared. Guv set off up the steps supporting one end of a table, with Jade and Jemma clutching the other.

'You bring the *little* things,' called Jade.

There weren't any little things. Cosy tugged at a roll of old carpet, musty-smelling and a bit damp. As she tugged, a spider suddenly raced out of the top of it, big as a soup plate with legs like tentacles. Cosy squawked and sprang for safety. The carpet fell, with a thud. The spider galloped off into the gloom.

Behind the carpet was another piece of furniture. It looked like a desk of some kind. Cosy approached it cautiously. It was a desk! It was *Kathleen's* desk!

Cosy pulled and tugged and hauled and panted, until at last she had managed to heave the desk out into the middle of the cellar floor. There, beneath the murky yellow glow from the naked bulb that hung from the ceiling, she eagerly examined it. Yes! It was! The very same desk! Old now, and battered, the surface covered in scratches and stains, but it was *the desk.*

The desk at which Kathleen Trimble had sat to write her journal, all those long, long years ago!

Cosy's heart began racing. She had found the Ghost Girl's desk! There was the little inkpot in the corner, in which she dipped her pen. It was empty, of course, but at the bottom, when Cosy took it out and held it beneath the light, she could still see signs of the ink that had once been there. A blue-black deposit. Kathleen had always used blue-black! And there was the runnel where she used to keep her pencils. And the big drawer underneath, in the middle. What had she kept in the drawer?

Holding her breath, Cosy eased the drawer out. It came stiffly, jerking on its runners. And oh, such a disappointment! It was bare! Completely bare, save for one small scrap of blue paper caught at the back.

Gently, Cosy teased it out. It looked as if it had been torn from the front cover of an exercise book. It had part of a label stuck on it: 'for Girls'. That must have been the school she went to.

Something School for Girls. Then her name, [Kathlee]n Trimble. Then the subject—'phy'. Geography? And her form—[Low]er IVB.

Cosy pressed the scrap of paper to her nose. It still smelt papery, and also a bit woody, from being shut in the drawer for so long.

She heard the voices of Jade and Jemma, shrieking as they came back through the house. Reverently, she folded the paper into a neat little envelope round the label and slipped it into the back pocket of her jeans. This was something that Kathleen Trimble had actually touched! Had actually *used*. Cosy pictured her filling in the label on the first day of term. Stuffing the book into her schoolbag when she had homework. Taking it home with her, back to 44 Alma Road.

Taking it up to her bedroom, laying it on her desk

'Hey! Tea Cosy!'

Jade and Jemma had come clattering back again, down the cellar steps.

'What you up to? Stop day-dreaming!'

'I'm not daydreaming! I've found something.'

'What?' Jade leapt forward. 'Pot of gold?'

'Headless body?'

'Precious jools?'

'I've found a desk,' said Cosy.

'*A desk?*' Jade's lip curled into a hoop. 'That old thing?'

'It'll clean up,' said Cosy. 'Guv!' She appealed to him as he appeared at the foot of the steps. 'Could we keep it? Could I have it?'

'No way!' Jemma grabbed at one corner of the desk. Jade grabbed at the other. 'Everything has to go!'

'Oh, stop!' begged Cosy. 'You'll break it!'

'What d'you want it for, anyway? Look at the state of it!'

'I've always wanted a desk,' said Cosy. 'Oh, Guv, please! Please say I can have it!'

'Well, of course you can if you really want,' said Guv. 'But she'll never let you take it upstairs in that condition. There's a lot of work needs doing on it.'

'I don't mind,' pleaded Cosy. 'I'll do it!'

'This ain't fair!' cried Jemma. 'Guv wasn't allowed to keep his bits of wood!'

Cosy's face fell.

'It's all right,' said Guv. 'I can live without my bits of wood. She can have the desk, if she's set her heart on it. There's no law says we have to junk everything.'

'In that case,' said Jemma. 'I'm gonna have something! I'm gonna have this bit o' carpet!'

Guv shook his head. 'It'll be rotten, for sure.'

'Well, so's her stupid desk,' said Jemma. 'Look at it!' She gave it a kick. 'Rickety old thing!'

The desk wasn't rickety, just stained and very dirty. Guv helped Cosy carry it out of the cellar and into the garden, where Auntie gave it the once-over and said, 'Yes, that's quite a find. That'll clean up a fair old treat!'

'Can I start on it right away?' said Cosy. She couldn't wait to get the desk upstairs and into her bedroom.

'Come and have a bite to eat,' said Auntie, 'then you can get cracking.'

'Yeah, an' we'll help, if you like,' said Jade.

'You what?' Jemma spun round, accusingly.

'I said, we'll help!'

'What do we have to help for?'

' 'Cos I say so!'

'It's only an old rubbishing bit of tat,' said Jemma.

'So what, if it's what she wants? It's for your homework, in't it?' Jade turned to Cosy for confirmation. Cosy nodded. 'Be a help, that will.'

'Don't see how,' grumbled Jemma.

'It don't matter how! She *wants* it.'

As soon as lunch was over the three of them, armed with polish and rags and buckets of soapy water, with sponges and brushes and a bottle of special stain remover, went into the back garden. Jemma was still inclined to sulk, but Jade remained firm: Cosy wanted the desk, so Cosy was going to have it.

In some ways Cosy would sooner have worked by herself because Jade did have rather a tendency towards bossiness. She wouldn't let Cosy do the job the way Cosy wanted to do it; it had to be done the way that Jade said.

'Needs scrubbing down first. Then we'll put the polish on. I'll do the top, you two get all the dust and bits out of them drawers.'

Jemma, still grumbling, and Cosy, rather more meekly, did what they were told. It was nice of Jade to help, thought Cosy, upending a drawer and banging on the bottom of it; she oughtn't to be ungrateful.

'Something in this one,' said Jemma.

'What?' Cosy sprang across to look.

'Sort of pen thing.'

'Oh!' Cosy made a dart at it.

'Hang off, snatch cat!' Jemma held the pen high up, out of arm's reach.

'Please!' implored Cosy.

It was Kathleen's pen—the one Cosy had seen her writing with. Red, with a funny kind of nib at the end, and teeth marks at the top where it had been chewed. Kathleen's teeth marks!

'Finders keepers!' chanted Jemma.

'Oh, look, just give it her!' roared

Jade.

'Why should I? I found it! Why should I let her have it?'

' 'Cos she wants it!'

'So do I!'

'What d'you want it for?' Jade looked at Jemma, scornfully. 'You never write nothing!'

Jemma sniffed and gave Cosy her pen. *I shall treasure this always*, thought Cosy. She wondered if she could find some ink to dip it in and whether it would still write.

By the end of the afternoon the desk was polished and gleaming. The worst of the stains and scratches were still there, but now it looked comfortably used rather than ramshackle. The three of them bore it triumphantly up the stairs to Cosy's room. Even Jemma had stopped grumbling and seemed prepared to regard their handiwork with a degree of pride.

'There! Looks real good,' said Jade when they had pulled out Cosy's homework table and fitted the desk in its place. 'Be all right now. You'll get straight *A*s for everything!'

Cosy giggled, nervously.

'You'd better!' said Jemma. 'After all this work we done!'

When Auntie and Guv had come upstairs and dutifully admired the new piece of furniture, and had taken the table back down—'It'll go nicely in your den,' said Auntie—they all trooped out to the kitchen for tea. Cosy was feeling quite weary at the end of such a hard day's labour, but still she was eager to get back upstairs and try out her new desk!

I won't start with maths, she thought. *I don't want to make myself miserable.*

Mrs Adie hadn't yet marked her last lot of algebra. Cosy was keeping her fingers crossed that thanks to the Ghost Girl she wouldn't be asked to stay behind again, but that was as much as she could hope for. With luck she might get a *C*, or a *C*+. But not even the Ghost Girl could turn her into a mathematical genius.

I'll do my English, she thought.

English was her favourite subject. Today they had to write a short story on 'Any subject of your choice'.

Cosy pulled up her chair. She sat, sucking the end of her pen. You couldn't chew a ballpoint like you could a pencil—or like Kathleen Trimble had chewed her dipping pen.

The dipping pen was made of wood. It lay now in the little runnel at the top of the desk. How strange it was to think of Kathleen, sitting in this very position, her elbows leaning where Cosy's leant, her eyes fixed in a faraway stare, at the window, just as Cosy's were. In Kathleen's day the window had had thick black curtains, because of it being wartime. It had been called the 'blackout'. Cosy had read about it in a book. She was glad they didn't have the blackout nowadays. It must have been horrible! Like living down a rabbit hole. You'd be scared to come out.

An idea suddenly rushed into Cosy's head. She snatched her pen out of her mouth and began to write.

'Once upon a time there was a rabbit called Jack. Jack Rabbit. He lived with his dad at the bottom of a burrow . . .'

Cosy wrote and wrote. She wrote ten

whole pages! She had never in her life written so much all in one go. By the time she had finished, and written THE END, very big and bold, her eyes were almost closing. A huge yawn engulfed her. She sank forward, her head resting on her arms. Before she knew it, she was fast asleep.

*   *   *

She was woken by the sound of Auntie calling up the stairs.

'Co-zee! Hot chocolate!'

Heavens! How long had she slept? It surely couldn't be bedtime already?

Cosy raised her head. She blinked. Where had her story gone? Her wonderful ten-page story!

Cosy's story had disappeared. In its place lay the Ghost Girl's journal. The Ghost Girl herself wasn't there, but the desk looked as if she had just that minute left it. The pen lay in its runnel, the nib new and shiny—and still wet with ink. Cosy eased herself up. There was ink in the inkpot!

Experimentally, she reached out a

hand and opened the long drawer where she had found the scrap of exercise book. The drawer was a jumble of stationery—rubbers, paper-clips, pencil sharpener, crayons, ruler, coloured chalks.

Cosy opened another drawer. This one was full of folders and exercise books.

She opened the third and saw a pencil case, a box of paints, a scrapbook, a photograph album. Cosy's hand itched to reach in and take out the photograph album! But she knew, if she tried, her fingers would only go straight through.

She did try, all the same. She couldn't resist it! But her fingers went through, just as she had known they would. And just like last time, they froze like lumps of ice.

Shivering, Cosy jammed her fingers into her mouth to warm them. She could touch the *desk*, because the desk was now part of the here and now. But not the things in it! The things in it still belonged to the past. It was so frustrating!

But the journal was there. She could read the journal.

Thursday
Well! This is it: the start of a new life. The school is to be evacuated and I am to go with it. We are leaving on Monday, first thing. I can scarcely believe it! Down to deepest Dorset . . . I am quite excited! Some of the girls are scared they will be homesick, but not me! Myra and Dinky are coming so we shall all be together and will have such fun. And no more nagging from Grandma! No more being crammed all night in that foul shelter, kept awake by her warthog snores.

While I am away I intend to work really hard and aim for good exam results so that not even Grandma will be able to say that staying on for Highers is a waste of time. I am going to become a doctor, no matter what! Nothing worthwhile is ever gained easily. Look at Florence Nightingale, how she had to fight! I know she was a nurse and not a doctor, but it was still a big struggle.

There is only one thing I regret, and that is that I shall no longer be here to

109

see my little ghosty person. She has been such a comfort to me! The knowledge that somewhere in time, but in this *VERY SAME PLACE WHERE I AM NOW*, she has existed and has been as miserable and frustrated as I so often am. Of course I am not happy that she is miserable, I would give anything to be able to cheer her up, but still it is a solace to know that one is not alone.

I once read somewhere that time does not flow in a straight line from A to B, the way we think of it, but is quite fluid. It can loop in a circle or bend back on itself and produce all manner of strange effects. I don't understand how it does this, but apparently it does. It is difficult for mere mortals to comprehend, being such 'straight line' creatures as we are. We live from birth to death, and after that we are at an end. Well, Grandma would not say so as she believes in an afterlife. I am not so sure; but in any event for all *PRACTICAL* purposes, in this world, we are at an end.

Wherever my little ghost person comes from, whether before me or even after me (for who knows?) it is as if there has *been a twist in time which has brought us together across the years.*

I would love to think that I would find her waiting for me when I came back! There are so many things I yearn to know. Such as, for instance, her algebra homework. Did she ever work out how to do it? Did she finally manage to get a good mark? I would like to think so. I cannot bear the thought of her being in trouble!

What is sad is that I have not even been able to have one last glimpse of her to say farewell. So I will say it now . . . Farewell, dear little ghost from across the years! I do so hope we meet again.

'Co*ZEE!*' Auntie's voice came booming up the stairs. 'Your chocolate's getting cold!'

Cosy pulled out her handkerchief and blew rather fiercely at her nose. Her Ghost Girl had gone! How could she exist without her Ghost Girl?

'Co-zee!'

Cosy trailed reluctantly to the door. 'Coming!'

She turned for one last glance, just in

case she might find Kathleen back at her desk, but of course she didn't; and now even the journal had gone. The pen was there, and the inkpot—but she bet there wasn't any ink in it.

She ran across and peered without much hope into the once murky depths. Sure enough, the little inkpot was bone dry. Decades, probably, had passed since there had last been any ink in it.

But back on the desk was Cosy's story. All ten pages of it! 'The Rabbit Who Stayed in His Burrow.' Cosy snatched it up and went charging downstairs, the story clasped in her hand. Auntie was in the kitchen, with Jade and Jemma. They were seated round the kitchen table, comfortable and fuggy in the heat of the old-fashioned stove. Jemma had a brown moustache from her hot chocolate.

'Well?' Jade looked at Cosy, challengingly. 'I hope you've bin working?'

'I have!' said Cosy.

'Did it make a difference, having a real desk?'

Cosy beamed. 'Yes! I did all this!' She waved the ten pages at them. 'It's a short story. Do you want to hear it?'

Jemma groaned.

'All right,' said Cosy, offended. 'I'll take it away again.'

'No!' Jade yanked at her arm. 'Read it to us.'

'Does she have to?' said Jemma.

'Yeah! She has to! I wanna know all our hard work was worth it. Go on!' She prodded at Cosy. 'Read!'

'But just drink your chocolate first,' begged Auntie. 'We don't want it going to waste!'

CHAPTER SEVEN

On Monday, Mrs Adie returned Year 7's algebra homework. Cosy had received a B+! She sat staring at it, her cheeks crimson. A warm glow, starting in her toes, went swirling upwards through her body. B+! For *maths*!

'That was really good, Cosy.' Mrs Adie was smiling at her. 'A great improvement! Did you do it all by yourself? No outside help?'

'Well—' Cosy was, on the whole, a truthful person. 'Someone showed me *how*, but they didn't actually *do* it.'

'That's all right! That's fine. So you think you've managed to grasp it at last?'

'Yes.' Cosy beamed. 'But only algebra,' she added, hastily. The Ghost Girl wouldn't be able to help her solve problems or fractions. The Ghost Girl had been evacuated. Down to deepest Dorset . . .

'Cosy, it all comes back to common sense,' said Mrs Adie. 'You've done it once, you can do it again.'

Last week at school had been a *bad* week. This week was going to be good! It just had that feel about it. At lunch-time Chloe Rowlands saved her a place right next to her at table, and afterwards, in the playground, a girl called Lottie Hamer came up and said, 'Do you want to hang out?'

Cosy said, 'Me?' Which was a stupid thing to say because who else could Lottie be talking about? There wasn't

114

anyone else there.

'You and me?' said Lottie.

'All right,' said Cosy.

'Come on, then!' Lottie tucked her arm through Cosy's and bore her away up the playground. 'Let's go!'

Cosy was even more pleased by Lottie wanting to hang out with her than she had been by Chloe saving her a place. Chloe might be the most popular girl in the class, but Lottie was way the most interesting. Well, Cosy thought so.

Lottie's real name was Charlotte. Most people called Charlotte would be known as Charlie, but Lottie wasn't a Charlie sort of person. She was a little gnomelike creature, with blue eyes like pebbles and brown hair tied into two sticky-out pigtails. People such as Michelle and Pandora jeered at her pigtails, but Lottie didn't care. She was what Mrs Pink would have called 'a law unto herself'. She was reputed to be fearsomely clever, but she wasn't at all serious or swotty. If any mischief was going on, you could be sure Lottie was at the bottom of it.

'We could be best mates,' she said to Cosy. 'If you want to, of course.'

Cosy gulped. Could this really be happening?

'I mean, you don't have to,' said Lottie. 'I just thought it might be fun. I've been keeping my eye on you,' she informed Cosy. 'See, I came up from Juniors so I already knew all the others . . . Chloe and Mich*elle* and Pan*dora.*' It was obvious that Lottie didn't think a great deal of Michelle or Pandora. 'So I looked at all the new girls and I picked on you.'

'Really?' said Cosy, trying to sound calm and casual.

'You seemed the most promising,' explained Lottie. 'Only at first I thought you were a bit too mousy. Then last week, *BOSH*!' Lottie slammed her right fist into the palm of her left hand. 'When you told Michelle to go boil herself! And then you told Pandora to naff off! Wow!' Lottie spun in a circle. 'That was really something!'

'I got into trouble for that,' said Cosy.

'Well, but you're not *living*,' said

116

Lottie, earnestly, 'till you've got into trouble! I've been in trouble so many times I've lost count. People that never get into trouble,' declared Lottie, 'are real drags. You *were* a drag—just a bit—but now you're OK. So it's you and me, man! If you'd like it to be.'

'I would!' said Cosy.

'Way to go!' cried Lottie; and she gave Cosy a companionable *biff* on the shoulder. 'We'll have to change desks; we need to sit next to each other. Do you want to come to the back or shall I come to the front?'

'I'll come to the back,' said Cosy.

Lottie nodded. 'A wise choice. All true individuals sit at the back.'

It was amazing what a difference it made, having a friend. Someone to giggle with, someone to whisper to, someone to share secrets. One day Cosy might even share the secret of the Ghost Girl. Not just yet; but one day.

The week went from good to even better. On Thursday, in English, Mrs Kemp gave them back their short stories.

'There's one I'd like to read out,' she

117

said. 'It's by Cosy Walker and it's called "The Rabbit Who Stayed in His Burrow".'

Cosy, from her new position at the back of the class, glowed like a bashful beacon as Mrs Kemp, in measured tones, read out her story.

'Once upon a time there was a rabbit called Jack. Jack Rabbit. He lived with his dad at the bottom of a burrow. The burrow did not actually belong to Jack and his dad, it belonged to a rabbit called Mrs Florence Bun, or Flo for short. Mrs Bun, being rather old and a bit stiff in the joints, lived at the top of the burrow. This saved her having to clamber up and down. Jack and his dad lived as deep as deep could be. Deep, deep, down in the earth, where it was safe and cosy.

'Jack's dad lived in the burrow both day and night. Jack couldn't remember the last time his dad had gone out. The outside world upset him, though he could never quite explain why. It just did.

' "It is one of those things," said Mrs

Bun.

'Jack went to school in a burrow two fields away, on the allotments. The school was called Rabbits and Hares Juniors. He took himself there and back every day. He had done this since he was a tiny bunny. His dad could not come with him because of not leaving the burrow and Mrs Bun was too old.

'On his way home from school Jack had to do the shopping. Also on Saturday mornings (though sometimes Mrs Bun did some for him). When Jack needed new clothes, Mrs Bun came with him to help him choose.

'On Sports Day at Jack's school, Jack was the only rabbit without any mum or dad (his mum having died when he was a mere baby). He felt really sad that his dad could not be there. Mrs Bun always came, but it was not the same.

'One year when Sports Day was coming up Jack grew rather angry. Why did his dad have to be different from other dads?

'"Couldn't you come just once?" he stormed. "It is only a short distance away, and Mrs Bun would be with you."

' "Now, Jack," said Mrs Bun, "don't nag your dad. You know he can't leave the burrow."

'But Jack's dad said, "It's all right, Flo. If it means so much to Jack, I will make a special effort just this once. I will go to his Sports Day."

'So he did, and Jack was so thrilled and excited that he won both the Bunny Hop and the Big Leap and was given a golden carrot! Unfortunately his dad was not there to witness it, as being in the outside world had proved too much for him and he had to be taken home, leaving Mrs Bun to congratulate Jack.

' "I'm so proud of you!" she said.

'His dad was proud, too, when Jack and Mrs Bun went home and told him the good news. But he was also ashamed.

' "You are a good son," he said. "I am sorry I am such a bad father."

' "You are not a bad father!" cried Jack. "I love you and I will look after you!"

' "It should be a dad who looks after his son," said Jack's dad; and his whiskers drooped and his ears flew at half mast.

' "Don't worry," said Jack. "Just because you cannot go out into the world does not mean we can't have fun at home."

'Jack and his dad had lots of fun! They played games together. They played Stoats and Adders and Hot Cross Bunnies and Oh, My Paws and Whiskers. Jack's dad helped Jack with his schoolwork and cooked him delicious meals, such as carrot crumble and salad stew.

'Jack vowed that never again would he nag at his dad and make him feel ashamed. What did it matter if he couldn't leave the burrow?

' "You are still the best dad in the world!" he cried.'

There was a silence as Mrs Kemp finished reading. Cosy wanted to curl up very small and hide under her desk. What would they think of her? They would think she was a baby! Writing about *rabbits.*

'Well!' said Mrs Kemp. 'Let's have some opinions! What did you think?'

'*Brilliant,*' said Lottie.

Cosy was her friend and she was going to get in first!

Maybe Lottie was just being loyal? Cosy waited, anxiously.

'Yeah.' That was Pandora. 'It was OK.'

'It was. It was great!'

One by one the others chimed in. They all agreed with Lottie! Even Michelle grudgingly admitted it was well written.

'I just don't understand why he never left the burrow.'

'Because he was scared!' snapped Lottie.

'Scared of what?'

'Life! The world! Everything!'

'Yeah, but—'

'You weren't *listening*!' cried Lottie. She had no patience with Michelle when she was being stupid. 'He's like those people you read about who suffer from agoraphobia and—'

'Aggra *what*?' said Michelle.

'Phobia!' screeched Lottie. 'It means they're scared of open spaces. They're scared of going *out.*'

'So what do they do?'

'They stay at home,' said Cosy.

'What, all the time? Never go out at all?'

'Weird!' said Pandora.

'It's like an illness. They can't help it,' said Cosy. 'It's not their fault.'

'So that's what this bunny has got? Aggra wotsit?'

'Phobia,' snarled Lottie. Under her breath she muttered, 'Moron!'

Mrs Kemp handed Cosy back her essay. 'Excellent work, Cosy! I'd like you to stay behind afterwards, if you would, and have a word with me.'

Well! At least this time she wouldn't be getting an order mark.

At the end of class the rest went trooping out ('I'll wait outside!' hissed Lottie) while Cosy, rather shyly, went up to Mrs Kemp's desk.

'Cosy, this was such a good story!' said Mrs Kemp. 'You must have enjoyed writing it. Did you?'

Cosy blushed, and nodded. (She did

wish she didn't blush so easily! It was such a silly, babyish habit.)

'I was wondering,' said Mrs Kemp. 'How would you feel about going in for the Junior Essay Competition?'

'Me?' gasped Cosy. She always found difficulty in believing that she could ever be singled out.

'Yes, you!' laughed Mrs Kemp. 'Why not? I wouldn't normally suggest it to a Year 7 girl, because after all you are still very new to the school, but this story is so exceptional . . . How would you feel about it?'

'I—' Cosy didn't know what to say.

'It's rather short notice,' said Mrs Kemp. 'The others have had since the beginning of term; you'll only have a couple of weeks. Which isn't really fair, but we do have half-term coming up . . .'

Mrs Kemp gazed down at Cosy. 'Let's leave it like this, shall we? Don't rack your brains, but keep an open mind. And if anything occurs to you— well! You write it down, and I'll put it in for the competition. You know the rules? There aren't many. The essay can be as long or as short as you like, but it has to be all your own work and it has to be on some subject connected with the school. That's all! Quite simple, you see. Go away and think about it, but don't get yourself in a frazzle. If you don't enter this year, there's always next.'

'What did she want?' demanded Lottie as Cosy came reeling out of the classroom.

'She wants me to go in for the Junior Essay Competition.'

'Wow!' Lottie's mouth dropped open. 'Nobody from Year 7 ever goes in for that!'

'I know, that's what Mrs Kemp said. So I wouldn't really stand a chance,' said Cosy.

' 'Course you would! She wouldn't have suggested it if she didn't think you stood a chance.'

'But I've only got two weeks and I can't think of anything to write about! It has to be something to do with school.'

'Hm . . .' Lottie ravelled her forehead into a mesh of lines. If she had been in a comic strip she would have had thought bubbles springing from her head. *Thinks . . .*

'I know!'

'What?'

'You could write about the school being bombed!'

'*Was* it bombed?' said Cosy.

'Yes! In the War. You don't think this is the original building, do you?'

Cosy had never really thought about it. 'I don't know much about the War,' she said.

'You don't have to. You could make it up!'

Cosy shook her head. 'I'm not very good at making things up.'

'You made up the rabbit story!'

Cosy fell silent. One day, perhaps, she would tell Lottie about Mum. Not just yet; but one day.

'I'll try and think of something,' she said.

In spite of Mrs Kemp telling her not to frazzle herself, Cosy almost squeezed her brain to a pulp in search of a subject for the essay competition. It was no use! She didn't have the right

126

sort of imagination. She could write only about things she knew.

*　　　*　　　*

Cosy was still frazzling and puzzling and squeezing her brain when Auntie greeted her one afternoon on her return from school with a triumphant beam.

'Guess what?'

'We've won the lottery!' yelled Jade. She threw her school bag into the air. 'Yippee!'

'I wish,' said Auntie.

'You mean we *haven't*?'

'Not quite that. But Cosy will be pleased. I've found someone for her!'

'For me?' said Cosy.

'Yes! Do you remember you wanted to know more about the people who lived in the house? Well, I've found someone who can tell you!'

'Oh.' Cosy tried to summon up the excitement that Auntie obviously expected her to feel. The truth was, she had been so bound up with the essay competition she had almost forgotten her interest in the house.

'I was talking to this old lady in the supermarket. She was complaining about the apples. Quite right, too! We had a long conversation about them. Taste like sawdust, modern apples. When I was young—'

Cosy caught Jade's eye. Jade pulled a face, and Cosy tried not to giggle.

'Anyway,' said Auntie, 'to cut a long story short, it turns out she lives just round the corner in Clyde Road.'

Clyde Road? That rang a bell! Wasn't Clyde Road where the Ghost Girl had said they had dropped a bomb?

'However, in the *War*—' Auntie brought it out with a flourish—'in the *War*, she lived just a few doors down, at number 56!'

'Gosh,' said Cosy. And then hurriedly, before Jade and Jemma could start mimicking her, 'Wow!' she added.

'I thought you'd be pleased,' said Auntie. 'She said if you want to go round and talk to her, you're quite welcome. But you'll have to look sharp because she's off tomorrow to stay with her daughter for a month.'

'Best go right away,' said Jade.

Cosy wriggled uncomfortably. She *was* still interested in knowing about the house—but she was shy when it came to talking with strangers!

'I could always come with you,' said Jade.

'That's a good idea!' Cosy looked at Jade, gratefully. With two of them, it would be fun. With just Cosy-on-her-own, it would be an ordeal. But then, of course, if Jade were going Jemma saw no reason she shouldn't go, as well. She sulked when Auntie said no.

'Why not? How come she gets to go and not me?'

' 'Cos I got in first!' said Jade.

'And three of you would be too many,' said Auntie. 'This is an elderly lady, remember. She doesn't want a crowd. Treat her gently! Don't bully her. Her name is Mrs Archer, by the way.'

'Must be as old as God,' said Jade as she and Cosy set off for Clyde Road. 'I mean, alive in the *War*.'

Cosy had been doing some arithmetic on her fingers. Kathleen Trimble had been nearly fifteen when her school had been evacuated. That must have been *at least* fifty years ago. No, more! The war had ended in 1945, and that was . . . Cosy's fingers worked, rapidly. Fifty-five years! So if Kathleen had been fifteen in, say, 1942, that would make her—

Cosy did more counting. Seventy-three! Kathleen Trimble would be seventy-three! It was a sobering thought.

Mrs Archer lived in a small block of flats. She seemed pleased to see the two girls.

'So nice,' she said, 'to find young people who have an interest in the past. No one has any sense of history these days! No one cares. It's all got to be new and modern. Like this prison cell.' She waved a hand round the tiny entrance hall of her flat. 'Such a grand old house used to stand here! It was bombed, you know, in the War, and they put up this concrete box in its stead.'

Cosy's heart beat faster. That must have been the house that Kathleen Trimble had talked about!

'Now, you want to know about number 44.' Mrs Archer led the way through to a neat sitting-room filled with china knick-knacks and photographs in glass frames. 'When I was a girl—sit down, sit down! Anywhere you like. When I was a girl, an old lady used to live there. Cross old stick she was. Mrs Trimble. We used to call her Mrs Tremble because that's what she made us children do!'

Cosy smiled, politely. Jade, trying hard, said, 'Trimble, Tremble. Yeah! That's good.'

'Was there anyone else in the house?' asked Cosy.

'Yes, I remember there was a girl called Kathleen. Mrs Trimble's granddaughter. Her parents had been killed early on in the War, and she came to live in Alma Road.'

'Were you friends?' asked Cosy, hopefully.

'Oh, no, dear! I was older than Kathleen. We went to the same school but I was in the fifth form, quite a great girl, when she was just a little tiddler in the lower third. You don't have lower third now, do you? It's all changed. What form are you?'

'Um . . . Year 7,' said Cosy.

'Year 7! It doesn't have the same ring, does it?'

Cosy agreed that it didn't.

'What school did you go to?' said Jade. 'Was it Hall Cross?'

'Oh, no! Hall Cross wasn't there in my day. It was the High School for Girls.'

Cosy nearly fell off her chair. 'The high school?'

'That's where Cosy goes,' said Jade. 'She got a scholarship.'

'Did you, indeed? Then you must be very clever. Like Kathleen. She was one of the clever ones.'

'I suppose you don't know what happened to her?' said Cosy.

Mrs Archer shook her head. 'I'm afraid I don't. The school was evacuated and Kathleen went with it, but I'd already left by then. That must have been . . . let me see . . . 1942. And before she came back I'd gone into the forces and was well away. Then at the end of the war—' Mrs Archer reached out a hand for one of her photographs—'I got married and went to live in Canada.'

She handed the photograph to Cosy. Jade peered at it over Cosy's shoulder. Mrs Archer, as a young bride, with her husband on their wedding day. Cosy tried hard to pretend an interest, but all she could think was, 'The high school! Kathleen Trimble went to the high school!'

'So I never really knew what became of her,' said Mrs Archer.

'She must have died,' said Cosy, sadly.

'Died?' Mrs Archer seemed surprised. 'Oh, no, dear! I don't think so.'

But she must have done, thought Cosy; or how could she be a ghost?

'I know the old lady went,' said Mrs Archer. 'My mother wrote and told me. But I don't remember her ever mentioning Kathleen. If she had been a casualty of war, I'm sure I would have

133

heard.'

'Maybe she died *after* the War.'

'But she was younger than I am!' Mrs Archer took her photograph back and stared at it, puzzled. 'Why should you think that she is dead?'

'Yeah.' Jade turned, accusingly, on Cosy. 'Why d'you keep on about her being dead all the time?'

'I—I don't know. I thought maybe . . . when the school was bombed—'

'But she was evacuated, dear! They all went down to Devon.'

'Dorset,' said Cosy, without thinking.

Jade pounced. 'How d'you know that?'

Cosy's cheeks fired up. 'A girl at school told me.'

'Well, it wasn't very interesting,' said Jade, as they walked back home, 'was it?'

'I thought it was,' said Cosy.

'But she didn't tell you nothing!'

'She did. She told me heaps! Especially the bit about the girl going to my school. That was *really* interesting.'

'Yeah. I s'ppose.' Jade didn't sound

very convinced. But then Jade didn't know Kathleen!

'I'm going to write an essay about her,' said Cosy, 'for the Junior Essay Competition.'

'How can you write an essay about her when you don't even know nothing?'

'Oh!' Cosy gave a little smile. 'I'll imagine it.'

Now that she had her subject, Cosy could hardly wait to get started! Unfortunately, as usual, she had stacks of homework to wade through, and by the time she had finished it was almost time for bed. Any minute and Auntie would be calling up the stairs that her hot chocolate was ready. Auntie liked to make a ritual, every night, of them all drinking hot chocolate in the kitchen.

Ruefully, Cosy laid down her pen. She would tackle her essay on Saturday, which was the beginning of half term. She knew exactly how she would start it:

This is a story about a real girl who was born long ago . . .

A Real Girl

This is a story about a real girl who was born long ago. She lived in my house and went to my school. Her name was Kathleen Trimble and she had to live with her grandmother because her parents had been killed in the War.

The War began in 1939 and finished in 1945. Great Britain was fighting the Germans and also the Japanese. Other countries were also fighting them, for example America, Australia and New Zealand. I am not sure how Kathleen's parents were killed but probably it was a bomb, as the Germans were always flying over from Germany and dropping bombs on towns and cities. We did the same to them. Many innocent people were killed, men, women and children, old people and young people, sick people and babies, and even animals. It was a time of great terror and destruction and I am glad I was not alive during it.

In my bedroom I have the very desk that Kathleen used to sit at! I know it is hers because in one of the drawers there was a scrap of blue paper torn from the

136

cover of an exercise book. There is part of a label on it. The label says:

for Girls

n Trimble

phy

er IVB

I have worked out that it must have been her GEOGRAphy book and that she was in LOWer IVB. And I now know which school she went to. It was . . . the High School for Girls!

I discovered this by speaking to an old lady called Mrs Archer, who lives just around the corner. When Mrs Archer was a girl she used to live in my road at number 56. That is only a few doors away. Mrs Archer was at school with Kathleen though not in the same form, as Mrs Archer was a few years older. She was in the fifth form when Kathleen started and so they did not really know each other very well but Mrs Archer was able to tell me a few things about her.

She told me, for instance, that old Mrs Trimble, Kathleen's grandmother, was rather stern and crabby. She was behind the times and made no attempt to bring herself up to date, as a result of which

137

she and Kathleen had many quarrels. Kathleen wanted to behave like a modern girl! Modern for that day and age is what I mean. She wanted to stay up late, like her friends did. She had two special friends. One was called Myra, the other was called Dinky. I think Dinky must have been a nickname. They were both at the high school with Kathleen.

Another thing Kathleen wanted to do was go to medical school and train to become a doctor. This was the cause of some of the bitterest quarrels with her grandmother, as her grandmother did not think that being a doctor was a suitable career for a girl. She did not really believe in girls having careers. Probably she wouldn't have minded so much if Kathleen had wanted to become a nurse. But she thought only men should be doctors.

This is another reason I am glad that I was not alive then! I do not personally want to become a doctor, as I am no good at maths or science, which I think you would have to be. Also I am rather ~~squee squa~~ squeamish and sometimes feel faint at the sight of blood. But I do

138

want to go to university! Kathleen's grandmother thought that further education was just a waste if you were a girl.

Mrs Archer said that Kathleen was one of the clever ones. This is why she was so determined to stay on and take her 'highers', which I think must have been the same as A levels today.

Sometimes when I sit at my desk that was Kathleen's desk I feel that I am really close to her. I almost feel that she is there with me, looking over my shoulder, trying to help me when I am struggling, for instance, with my maths homework. I like to imagine that my bedroom was her bedroom. I picture her sitting at the desk, leaning her elbow where I am leaning mine, and chewing on the end of her pen for ~~insper~~ inspiration.

I have her pen as well as her desk! We discovered the desk down in the cellar, all scratched and stained and covered in cobwebs. It must have been there for a really long time, maybe ever since the end of the war. We carried it upstairs to clean and polish it and it was while we were doing this that I found the pen. It was in one of the drawers. I was so ~~exit~~ excited! It is nothing much to look at, just a wooden stick, painted red, with a nib at the end of it. But the tip of the wooden stick has teeth marks round it where it has been chewed! I like to imagine Kathleen nibbling on it while she ~~puzled~~ puzzled over a piece of homework or what to write in an essay.

The reason I am convinced it must have been hers is that it is a very old-fashioned type of pen, the sort that has to be dipped into ink, and in one corner of the desk there is a little pot that is stained bluey-black and smells all inky even now.

As I do my homework every night I like to picture Kathleen doing hers, gazing up at the window just as I do—except that in Kathleen's day there would have been thick curtains to keep the light from getting out. This was called 'the blackout' and everyone had to do it, it was a law. It was to stop the German pilots from seeing where to drop their bombs.

In spite of the blackout, however, the bombs kept falling. Where Mrs Archer *lives in her block of flats there was once a big old house that had a bomb dropped on it. Mrs Archer says it was very grand, unlike the concrete box that was put up in its place. Mrs Archer complains that no one has any sense of history these days. Everything has to be 'new and modern'.*

I find it very hard to imagine Kathleen being grown up and an old woman. I wonder if SHE would complain about everything being new and modern? Even though I cannot picture her as being old I can see her very clearly as a young girl. She would have worn the school uniform that was worn in those days, that is a white blouse with a tie, and a navy skirt coming down past the knees. It would have been considered indecent in those days for schoolgirls to wear short skirts! I think she would have had long hair, maybe tied back with a ribbon, or in a plait, because we are still not allowed to wear our hair flapping round our faces so I am sure in Kathleen's day they would not have been allowed to either.

I think about Kathleen so much I almost feel that I know her. At moments

141

when I have been sad or lonely, or unable to do my maths homework, I have felt that she was here with me, trying to cheer me up, and it has made me feel stronger and more determined, just like she was. You cannot simply give up, but have to battle through. That is what knowing Kathleen has taught me.

In 1942 the school was evacuated to deepest Dorset and Kathleen went with them, which was just as well, as later on the school was hit by a bomb and that is why today we have a modern building. By that time Mrs Archer had already left, and by the time that Kathleen came back she had gone away. At the end of the war Mrs Archer married and went to live in Canada. Her mother wrote to her that old Mrs Trimble, Kathleen's grandmother, had died but she never said anything about Kathleen and Mrs Archer does not know what became of her.

I cannot help wondering! It is like losing a friend and not knowing whether she is alive or dead. Was she killed in the war? Or did she manage to persuade her grandmother to let her go to medical school and become a doctor? I would

love to think so! But alas, I think I have to face the fact that I shall probably never know. All I can do is say goodbye.
Goodbye, my friend from long ago!

Written by Cosima Walker, Year 7

Cosy laid down her pen. That was it. Her essay. Finished! Now all she had to do was write it out neatly, in her best hand, checking for any spelling mistakes and making sure all the commas and full stops were in the right places.

She felt rather weary, but it was a good weariness. But it had made her sad, as well, because it *was* like saying goodbye. She had this feeling that Kathleen had gone, and she would never see her again. If only there were some way she could have thanked her for the help she had given Cosy with her algebra homework! Kathleen had been so anxious to know whether she had done well. If only she could write her a note!

Well, and why shouldn't she? Cosy leaned forward and snatched back her pen.

Dear Kathleen,
I am the girl from the future that you have written about in your journal. I think you would like to know that I got a B+ for my algebra!!! Thank you for helping me.
P.S. I do hope you manage to become a doctor!

It was silly, of course. For how did she imagine that Kathleen would ever be able to read it? All the same . . .
I'll leave it on the desk, thought Cosy. *Just in case.*

CHAPTER EIGHT

The Ghost Girl never did come back. For a long while, Cosy really missed her. Every time she sat at her desk she expected to feel her hovering at her side or peering over her shoulder. Every time she struggled with her maths homework she thought about

144

her. Every time she came upstairs to bed she held her breath in the hope of finding her there, writing in her journal. But it never happened, and after a bit Cosy stopped looking.

She didn't forget about Kathleen, she would never forget about her! But suddenly life was busy and full. Busier than it had ever been.

This was mainly because of Lottie. At Lottie's insistence, she joined the after-school book club, which met once a week on a Tuesday to swap books and discuss which were their favourites. She auditioned for the junior choir and could hardly believe it when she was accepted. (Cosy, who had always thought she couldn't sing a note!) She was picked for the under-13 netball team, which meant staying behind on a Friday for practice.

One Saturday she was invited back to Lottie's place for tea, and then the following Saturday, Lottie came to Alma Road. Cosy, full of anxieties, had worried that Jade and Jemma might think Lottie a little too posh, or too brainy, and that Lottie might be put off by Jade and Jemma's double act. They could be overpowering if you weren't used to them. But Lottie could give as good as she got, and the Terrible Two, as Auntie called them, quite liked people who stood up for themselves.

After tea they went upstairs to play Catwalk. Cosy was a bit nervous, just at first, in case clever Lottie considered the game beneath her. It *was* rather childish and silly, thought Cosy. But Lottie could be just as childish and silly as anyone! It was Lottie who stripped the pillowcases off the pillows and made pillow case hats for herself and Cosy. It was Lottie who took down the curtains and gigglingly wrapped herself up in them—and then fell off the catwalk because she could hardly move one foot in front of the other.

'What on earth has been going on?' said Auntie, as they trooped back downstairs.

'*She* got caught in the curtains,' said Jemma.

'Well!' Auntie shook her head. 'That's a new one!'

'I like to be original,' said Lottie.

Cosy gazed upon her friend with quiet pride. Not even Jade and Jemma could get the better of Lottie!

*   *   *

Towards the end of November, Miss Marriott told Cosy that she had at last managed to arrange for her to visit her mum.

'Next Friday, after school. I'll pick you up and we'll go there together.'

Cosy was excited—of course she was!—at the thought of seeing Mum again, but she was just a little bit anxious, as well. Cosy spent a lot of her life being anxious.

'Don't worry,' said Lottie. 'It'll be all right!' Cosy had told her about Mum, though not about the Ghost Girl. 'Stands to reason . . . they wouldn't let you go and see her if she wasn't getting better.'

Lottie was never anxious about anything. Nor were Jade and Jemma.

'Just think of lots of good things to tell her,' urged Jade.

'Yeah! Things that'll make her

147

happy.'

'Make her wanna come home.'

'Like what?' said Cosy.

Jade looked at Jemma: Jemma looked at Jade. They rolled their eyes.

'Like playing Catwalk,' said Jemma.

'Like finding the desk.'

'Like being in the netball team.'

'Like—'

'Oh!' Cosy clapped a hand to her mouth. 'I'll have to miss netball practice!'

'*Oh,*' said Jade.

'*Oh,*' said Jemma.

'*What a disaster!*'

'Miss Beale doesn't like you to miss netball practice,' muttered Cosy.

But of course Miss Beale didn't mind, when Cosy explained the reason.

'Good heavens, Cosy! Don't apologize. Not even I would claim that a netball practice is more important than visiting your mum!'

Cosy had longed to be with Mum; she had dreamt of nothing else. Now the moment had come and here was Cosy getting herself into a dither. She couldn't help being apprehensive. She hated seeing Mum in hospital. There were so many sad-looking people there. Old ladies shuffling down the corridor in shapeless dresses and fluffy bedroom slippers. Old men sitting staring into space. Women of Mum's age being helped along by nurses, their eyes glazed and empty. Even, sometimes, *young* people.

Cosy found it quite frightening. She was always terrified that one day Mum would go into hospital and not come out. That one day Cosy would go to visit and it would be Mum who was shuffling down the corridor or staring into space.

'Try not to fret yourself, love!' Auntie put an arm round Cosy's shoulder and gave her a hug. 'Your mum's on the mend. She'll be back with you before you know it!'

Then Mrs Pink rang up in great excitement.

'Cosy! Guess what! I had a call from your mother! She sounded almost like her old self. I've told Jonathan you'll be back by Christmas!'

'Do you think I really will?' Cosy

looked hopefully at Miss Marriott as they drove to the hospital.

'We'll see,' said Miss Marriott. 'We'll see.'

*   *   *

It wasn't until Cosy was clasped in Mum's arms, her head buried in Mum's shoulder, that she really began to believe Mrs Pink might be right. She did hope so! Jonathan would be so disappointed.

And then Mum said, 'Darling, there's something I have to tell you. I want you to be very, very brave!' and Cosy's heart immediately sank.

'What is it?' she whispered.

'I was hoping the doctors would let me come home this week, but they say I've got to stay here a while longer.'

'How much longer?' whispered Cosy.

'I might have to stay until Christmas.'

'Christmas?' cried Cosy. A great flood of relief washed over her.

'Yes.' Mum looked at her, anxiously. Mum, like Cosy, was a very anxious person. 'Do you think you could bear to go on living with the Ridleys until then? It's not so very long! Only just a few weeks. It will soon pass! You could make a special calendar and tear off the days. And maybe when school finishes you could go and help Mrs Pink with the Christmas shopping . . . You could buy a tree! You could buy a Christmas tree, Cosy, and decorate it for me! For when I come home. Could you do that, do you think?'

Cosy nodded, solemnly. 'Yes. I could do that.'

'And you wouldn't mind too much? Staying with the Ridleys for just a little while longer?'

'I wouldn't mind,' said Cosy, 'not now that I know you're coming home. I didn't like it too much at first. I kept crying all the time 'cos I missed you so.'

'Oh, Cosy! Sweetheart. I'm so sorry!'

'No, it's all right,' insisted Cosy. She didn't want to make Mum feel bad. 'I've got over it. I mean, I still miss you, but I don't keep crying all the time. I've learnt to be strong.'

'Yes,' said Mum, 'and I am learning

151

to be strong, too!'

When Jade and Jemma heard that Cosy would be leaving them at Christmas they both pulled faces.

'Just as we'd got used to you,' grumbled Jade.

'Won't be able to play Catwalk!' said Jemma.

'We will,' said Cosy, ' 'cos I could come round and see you. Or—' She stopped, and her face grew pink.

'Or what?' said Jemma.

'You could come round and see me! I could ask Lottie, as well, and we could have a party. Just the four of us.'

'Yeah!' Jemma punched the air.

'Good idea,' said Jade. 'And we'll bring the catwalk!'

*   *   *

The last week of term arrived and so did Speech Day, when all the school gathered in the Big Hall, along with parents and brothers and sisters, to listen to the headmistress's report, and to the guest speaker, and to watch the prizes being handed out.

The speaker this year was someone called Professor Kaye Lavenham. Nobody had heard of her, and she was rather old, and Cosy's form, for the most part, quickly decided that she was of no interest whatsoever.

'Just some boring old dodderer,' said Michelle. 'Where *do* they dig them up from?'

'Last year—' Lottie hissed it at Cosy as they filed in to take their places— 'they had Elizabeth Allysson. You know? The *writer*? Just my luck! I would have loved to see her. Oh, look!' She nudged at Cosy. 'There's my parents . . . that's my mum, in the blue coat.'

Cosy looked—and looked again. Her jaw dropped open. Sitting further along the row, just two or three places away from Lottie's mum in her blue coat, was . . . *Cosy's* mum! Cosy's mum, wearing cheerful bright red and looking trim and pretty. And by her side was Mrs Pink, hair specially puffed up and blue-rinsed for the occasion.

Cosy's heart nearly burst with a great explosion of love. Mum had made this

153

effort specially for her! Mum, who was so scared of the outside world. And darling Mrs Pink had come with her, to give her courage!

'Hey!' Lottie was tugging at Cosy's sleeve. 'Sit down! Everyone's looking at you.'

Cosy promptly collapsed on to her seat. She didn't want to be looked at!

Speech Day began. In places it was quite fun, like watching members of the sixth form go up to receive their prizes, all dressed in their best clothes because unlike the rest of the school they didn't have to wear school uniform. Lottie kept buzzing little comments into Cosy's ear.

'Dowdy!' or '*No* dress sense' or 'She could play Catwalk!'

But parts of it, Cosy had to admit, were a little bit draggy, especially when the chair of governors got up and talked and talked and didn't ever seem likely to stop, but Cosy was so thrilled about Mum being there that she really didn't mind too much.

'And now,' announced Mrs Latymer, the headmistress, 'I am honoured to

154

present our guest speaker, Professor Lavenham.'

Everyone clapped, politely.

'Professor Lavenham,' said Mrs Latymer, 'is one of our old girls, so we are especially proud to have her with us on this occasion. Before handing over, I should just like to take the opportunity of thanking both the Professor, for so generously giving of her time, and our own Old Girls' Association, who did such a splendid job of tracing her . . . because, you see, there is a very special reason for the Professor being here tonight.'

Mrs Latymer and the Professor exchanged smiles.

'You will learn in a moment what that special reason is. I don't intend to spoil it by telling you myself, I'll leave that to our guest. Professor Lavenham!'

Lottie pressed her mouth to Cosy's ear: '*Bor*ing!'

Cosy nodded, dreamily. She wasn't really taking very much notice. She was thinking about Christmas . . . about the tree they would have and the

155

decorations she would put up. And the present she would buy for Mum. What could she buy? Something that Mum would really treasure. Something—

She became aware that Lottie was digging her in the ribs. Cosy snapped to attention.

'. . . Junior Essay Competition,' said the guest speaker. 'Third prize goes to Jenny Geary, in Year 8, for her essay entitled "A Typical School Day".'

The school clapped politely as Jenny Geary bounced up to the stage to receive her certificate and book token.

'Second prize goes to Amy Barratt, Year 9, for "Elysian Fields".'

Clap, clap, clap, went Cosy, dutifully. There wasn't any point her heart thudding and banging. She wasn't going to win. How could a Year 7 hope to compete with a Year 9?

'First prize—' Professor Lavenham paused. 'Before I announce the winner of the first prize, I just wanted to say a few words about the essay that she wrote.'

Lottie groaned. Even Cosy thought it was a bit much. Who wanted to hear about the rotten old essay? Just say who wrote it and put everyone out of their misery!

'This essay is about a girl who was at the High School for Girls many years ago—during the war, in fact.'

Cosy's cheeks began one of their slow burns. Butterflies fluttered in her stomach.

'Is that yours?' hissed Lottie.

Was it? Could it be? No! Loads of people had probably written about girls who had been at the school during the war.

'The girl's name,' said Professor Lavenham, 'was Kathleen Trimble.'

Cosy's heart almost stopped beating.

'It *is* yours, isn't it?' whispered Lottie.

Cosy gulped, and nodded.

'She lived with her grandmother and it was her great ambition to go to medical school and become a doctor.'

Professor Lavenham paused. 'I was that girl! I was Kathleen Trimble.'

Cosy sat, rigid. Professor Lavenham was Kathleen Trimble? *She* was the Ghost Girl?

'I did go to medical school—and I did become a doctor! But I got married and changed my name to Lavenham, and I'd always loathed the name Kathleen, *loathed* it! So I became Kaye, instead, because that was what my friends all called me. And now, all these years later, I have been written about in an essay—by a girl who found my desk down in her cellar!'

Lottie shot a quick glance at Cosy.

'You never told me all this!'

'I know,' whispered Cosy.

'Anyway—' Professor Lavenham smiled; and suddenly, just for a moment, in spite of the grey hair and the wrinkles, she looked like the Kathleen whom Cosy remembered. 'That's quite enough of me! I mustn't keep you in suspense any longer. The winner of the first prize is . . . Cosima Walker, from Year 7! Come on up here, Cosy.' Professor Lavenham beckoned. 'Come and get your prize!'

On wobbly legs, amidst a storm of applause—never in the school's history had anyone from Year 7 won the Junior Essay Competition!—Cosy made her way up to the stage. Shyly, she shook hands with Professor Lavenham. With the Ghost Girl! She was shaking hands with the Ghost Girl!

'Very well done,' said Professor Lavenham. 'I read about myself with huge enjoyment! I was amazed you could—you could . . .'

Her voice faded. She looked down at Cosy. There was puzzlement in her eyes—and just a hint of recognition.

The hall fell silent. It was a silence that seemed to last for ever.

'The girl from the future!' Professor Lavenham's hand closed over Cosy's, holding it very tight. 'I was so glad to hear you got a B+ for your algebra homework!'

*   *   *

'What was all that about?' hissed Lottie, as Cosy went dancing back, light-hearted, to her seat.

'Oh . . . nothing, really,' said Cosy.

But Lottie was her friend. Her very, very *good* friend! You didn't keep secrets from friends. Lottie deserved to know.

'I'll tell you later,' whispered Cosy. 'Promise!'